T0147305

A Runway
For A Dream

A story of a dream and the transition
in a girl's life to make it a reality

CLAIRE GILBERT

iUniverse, Inc.
New York   Bloomington

A Runway For A Dream
A story of a dream and the transition in a girl's life to make it a reality

iUniverse books may be ordered through booksellers or by contacting:

iUniverse
1663 Liberty Drive
Bloomington, IN 47403
www.iuniverse.com
1-800-Authors (1-800-288-4677)

ISBN: 978-1-4502-3577-8 (pbk)
ISBN: 978-1-4502-3578-5 (ebk)

Printed in the United States of America

iUniverse rev. date: 7/14/2010

Chapter 1
THE HERITAGE

Erika was so delighted with her new home that she walked over to look out of the window in the living room to check the surroundings outside. She was so happy that she had found this apartment and at the rent she could manage on her small budget. Thinking of that, Rod Burton, the man who rented it to her, came into her mind. He was so handsome and seemed like a sweet, compassionate man who wanted to help her by giving her a rent amount that he felt she could manage. He seemed so concerned with her welfare and said that he would be stopping by to check on her. Would he really do that, she asked herself?

Checking out the surroundings on the outside, she could hear the laughter and noises of the children playing in the park across the way. She was aware of how pretty and colorful they were dressed. Their clothing was so colorful, almost like what she had seen in rainbows

It was unusual for her, coming from the Amish, farming country where she had lived all of her life while growing up. They didn't use bright colors back there, and were very conservative with their dress codes.

Everything and everybody seemed to be moving fast here. She wondered if she would become accustomed to all of this, then decided she must, if she was to follow her childhood dream. This was a very big city, and she had never been to a big city, never been away from her home or the Amish life that she was raised by, before coming here.

Watching the children with their colorful clothing, she remembered that the colors back where she was from, didn't seem to be colors at all but were tones of beiges and grays and very drab.

She concluded that her life style would need to be different now that she had come to this big city to fulfill her dream. Everything was much different here compared to what she was used to seeing where she came from. Being brought up in a small farming town near Lancaster, Pennsylvania, by an Amish family with their religious beliefs certainly didn't prepare her for this type of life.

Standing there awhile she began to reminisce, her thoughts went back to her childhood and her life before she came to this big city.

Her heritage was traced back hundreds of years to when her ancestors migrated to the United States in the late seventeen hundreds from the French area of Alsace-Lorraine. Despite all the time that had passed and the many changes that had taken place in society, they still lived and worked as their forefathers did. They were devout in their faith and maintained the Amish way of living and habits. Most of these settlements were very rural and farming lands.

She remembers playing games and romping with the other Amish children at a young age, just as the children she is watching are doing. She thought of the hard life her parents had working in the fields as did everyone they knew in that area. This was what they wanted and believed that would keep them close to God. Even the children were required, helping and learning to farm as they were growing up. They had long preferred the farming and trading as their livelihood. They would trade with other Amish families and sell what they farmed or made by hand. Trading between families and working in the fields was everyone's way of life.

Her family consisted of her mother and father and three older brothers: James, David and Seth; and a younger sister, Rachel.

Thinking about how her father tilled the fields with only a plow drawn by horses, which was the general practice among these people.

And that didn't seem unusual to them. He also raised cattle for milk and farmed hay and crops of corn, soybeans, and grains—whatever they needed for food that they wouldn't need to purchase. These were some of the things going through her mind as she stood there.

She remembers the one-room school that she attended with the other children where all the grades up to the eighth grade were all in one room and how they had to walk to school. If the weather was too bad, they were driven by horse and buggy.

She could see her mother, her sister Rachel and herself doing all the domestic work like cleaning, cooking and baking, and whatever sewing they could do to earn extra money as income. The brothers were required to work in the fields and help with man's work. Sometimes when more help was needed, the women joined in also.

At harvest time, they would trade or sell their products to other farmers or to the towns- people nearby. That was how most of them existed. They would also have fairs and roadside stands to sell their products which would consist of livestock, hay, grains and any other produce that they could harvest. The women were well known for their delicious bakery goods and their sewing crafts, and also the beautiful quilts that they made by hand.

When they had the opportunity to make different kinds of crafts by hand, they would make up many and sell them. Their customers were the travelers and visitors to the area and the people from the surrounding towns. The buyers appreciated their purchases because they could see that they were meticulously made by hand.

From the time that she could remember, she had a passion for drawing wearing apparel, and as she grew older, she became interested in drawing different types of attire for the girls, but they often could not wear them because of their old beliefs. She was never very happy with the type of clothing they had to wear.

The clothing for the women was so drab looking. All the women were required to wear the same type of garments. They were very loose-fitting long dresses. Most of them were made by hand and from flour sacks with no color, and they wore an apron over them also made of flour sacks of dark drab colors. It made her feel inferior when the people would come to their fairs to shop and she would notice their beautiful attire.

As she grew, she would ask her mother if she could bake some things and sell them at the fairs and roadside stands and also sell some of the pretty crafts that she made. Her mother agreed because their people believed in creativity and crafts, and she was very successful in selling them. After being successful in her sales, she asked to be allowed to save the money she was making for her items. She told her mother that she would save it for her future. Her mother agreed to that, if she would continue to help at home with the chores.

She loved to sell her things. She would sew little craft things and bake pastries that were different and watch the people being pleased with them.

When the Amish had their fairs, people came from all over, and she would notice the nice clothing the girls wore and envied them. She was never happy with her life, even though she loved her parents and siblings. She thought that everything was drab, and she always dreamed of having something better. She hated wearing those big, loose dresses and aprons that her mother made by hand from flour sacks and shoes that looked like they were for men.

She continued to spend a lot of her spare time drawing things she thought she would like to see as their dresses. Her father always tried to discourage her. He said, "Thee might be better off if thee worked in the fields. The drawing will never give any benefit to thee; it will never be of any use to thee."

But Erika loved her drawings. She kept thinking—when I get older I will make use of it. I will start right now to save what money I earn and later go to a school where I can learn more about fabric and clothes and fashion.

She never failed to ask her mother if she could bake and make up some pretty craft items to sell at the fair, so that she could put the money into her savings. She enjoyed baking delicious cakes and cookies and design pretty little crafts out of material left over from her mother's quilts, and when she sold them, the money went into her savings.

Erika remembers, at one of these fairs when she was about thirteen years old, she met a girl who was visiting the fair with her parents, and she was to become her very close friend. Her name was Darcy. While she visited the fairs, she and Darcy talked and exchanged many of the family customs in their different lives. They liked each other and found that they had many ideas in common.

Erika had a pretty face with beautiful, long, blonde hair that cascaded over her shoulders, when it wasn't necessary to be tied up in her Amish hat, and she was very tall and slender although no one could see that, as she wore long, very loose dresses as did all the Amish girls. She was a very pretty girl.

Darcy was not as tall as Erika but also very pretty with a nice, slender figure that was visible with the dresses she wore, and her hair was a chestnut color in a medium length.

Thinking about it now, she remembers Darcy being there every time there was a fair, which occurred two or three times a year depending on the weather. After a couple of years, they became very close friends. Darcy thought Erika was very talented with her art. She understood what Erika wanted in her life. She would often bring fashion magazines to Erika, which she would hide from her parents because she knew they would not approve of her reading them. She would use them to guide her in the designs that she was working on.

Bringing Darcy to mind, she remembered how their friendship grew all during grade school. When Erika was about fifteen and a half years of age, Darcy enrolled in the high school in Lancaster, and she asked Erika if she thought she could persuade her parents to allow her to attend that school also.

Erika told her that this would be a very difficult thing to do as it was not the Amish belief to further school education beyond the eighth grade. They believed in teaching domestics and farming in the home after that time. She told Darcy that her parents would consider the school too worldly, but she would try. She did try and it was a very long struggle, but after much pleading, they finally, reluctantly agreed.

Her father was not happy about it at all and said to her, "Thee will be very odd among other children with thy Amish appearance."

"I will accept that father," she replied. "I understand there will be other Amish children attending that school and perhaps they will be dressed like me." She answered. She never found any other Amish students in that school.

When her father agreed, he told her he would need to take her to school in the horse and buggy, but she didn't mind as long as she could attend that school with Darcy.

During the time she attended that school she still continued with her fashion drawings. She decided to set her sights on a design institute to further her fashion education.

When the knowledge of her fashion drawings became known to the students, she started to acquire requests to design and make prom gowns for the senior students and her savings continued to build. She was very grateful that her mother allowed her to do this at home; she also helped her with the sewing. Her mother approved of her designing crafts and arts. The Amish believed in letting their people have crafts, and many of them were known for their beautiful handmade quilts and other things, which they sold at the fairs as Erika's mother did.

Erika knew then, that she would follow her dream to be a fashion designer no matter what. She told Darcy she would find a special school to attend, to pursue her knowledge and desires. Whenever Darcy brought the fashion magazines to her, she would search through them and look for all the fashion information.

Once, when she was looking through a magazine, she saw an advertisement for a fashion design and art institute, and she made a note of it. She planned right then to inquire about that and later find out where it was located. So she continued with her schooling and with designing and fabricating clothes to build up her savings.

When graduation time for her and Darcy arrived, she got a lot of requests for designer prom gowns and started on them as soon as she could. Then she decided to take some of her savings and buy a sewing machine to help her, as it would save time. It was just a treadle operated machine but it was an improvement over sewing by hand

The students would select one of her designs that they liked, purchase their own fabrics and bring them to Erika to fabricate. Her mother gave her a lot of credit for her determination and how she was building up her savings and helped her all she could. That kept her busy and she added more to her savings. She became more anxious to follow her dream. She remembered the ad in the magazine about the art and fashion design institute and was determined to check it out.

After graduation, her friend Darcy had gotten a job with a department store in Lancaster selling lingerie and told Erika that if she would leave the area, Darcy would think about going with her as soon as she had enough money saved up.

When Erika had passed her nineteenth birthday, in her mind, she was ready to go, but her parents were not happy about her leaving. They asked her to stay until she was a few years older as they were afraid for her safety out in the world. To please them and make them more at ease, she agreed to stay until her twenty-first birthday. But she was very determined and concentrated on building her savings up further. In that time she knew she could build up her savings to a very nice amount.

She kept very busy with her designing and sewing, and she continued to help her mother as much as she could, but her heart was drifting toward New York and her career.

Then she decided that she would make some new dress clothes for her trip as she felt that her present wardrobe would attract too much attention and curiosity in the wrong way, and she would feel out of place. She became busy planning to get that finished in time.

When she passed her twenty-first birthday and on her way to became twenty-two, she made her definite plans and decided she would leave right after her next birthday in February of 1945. She talked it over with her parents and told them it was time for her to go.

So when February of the next year came around and winter was moving away, she felt she was ready to go.

Her parents were not very happy about losing her to the big city, and her sister felt sad to hear of her leaving. Erika consoled her by telling her that when she came of age, she could come to New York also if she desired.

She loved her parents and family, but she had this determination to follow her dream.

Now she had over three thousand dollars saved and felt that would get her started. It sounded like a lot of money to her, at that time. She was very sure that she would find some kind of a job to support herself when she got to New York.

She talked to Darcy and they made plans to go together. Erika would go first and find a place to live, and Darcy would follow as soon as she had a little more money.

Never having been to a big city before, she decided she would check with many people about where in New York to go initially and if they could give her some direction. One of Erika's school friends told her that her mother used to live there and would answer her questions. The mother's advice was to take the bus to Brooklyn or Queens because there she would have a better chance of getting an affordable room or apartment.

So she began to make her plans according to that advice. The more she planned, the more excited she became. She could hardly wait for the day to come when she would purchase her bus ticket.

It was right after her twenty-second birthday in March of 1945 when she finally purchased her bus ticket to Brooklyn and prepared to leave. She felt sure that she had enough money to tide her over until she could get a job there. So with a very sad departure from her parents and siblings, she bid them farewell and said she would contact them as soon as she was settled. She also told Darcy she would contact her as soon as she found a place to live.

She was required to board the bus early in the morning—it was to be an overnight trip. This was to be a first for her. She had never been on a bus before. She had always traveled by horse and buggy.

The trip was rather an interesting one for Erika. Everyone on the bus seemed very pleasant and friendly. She was seated next to a very nice Jewish lady from Brooklyn. Her body seemed to take up most of the seat as she was almost as broad as she was tall, but she was very friendly. She had been visiting relatives in Lancaster and had all kinds of inquiries about the Amish people. Erika quizzed her a lot about New York, which she found very enlightening and was glad to be informed about the place that she was headed for. Some of the answers made her a little leery, but knew she had to go on.

Early the next morning just as the sun was coming up, the bus pulled up at the bus depot in Brooklyn. She was a little apprehensive to be in this strange, big city, but the tasks of finding a place to live and a job were the utmost in her thoughts.

She alighted from the bus wondering what step to take first. Deciding she had better find a place to live first, then a job—those would be her priorities. She knew she had to be very careful with her money as her savings had to last until she got a job.

She began to walk around in the bus depot and tried to observe everything. Then noticing a bulletin board with a lot of notes pinned on it, she started to read the notes. After reading all of them, she found that there were several with places for rent. She jotted down some of them to check on. Listed were a few rooms for rent at reasonable prices and one apartment that had no price.

After obtaining directions from a man in the depot, she started out. Taking a cab, she looked at the rooms first because she thought they would be more affordable. All of the rooms were in close proximity to the bus depot. One room was a dingy little room near a railroad track, and the next one was a shabby, dirty room in a rooming house at the end of a dark, smelly hallway. The rents were very cheap, but Erika felt she could not give in to them. She hoped this was not the type of living that she was going to find here in this big city, but she was determined not to let it discourage her,

Finally, she decided to just take a look at the small apartment, thinking the rent would probably be more than she could afford, but she wanted to look at it. She asked directions to where it was located and was told it was near Prospect Park and she would need transportation there. She motioned for a cab again and he took her searching for the location. When the cabby discovered the address, it was in a fairly nice area and it seemed to her that it should be in this tri-level building that she was looking at.

She got out of the cab, and the cabby asked her if she wanted him to wait but she said, "No thank you," paid her fare, and went up to the entrance of the building.

She entered the lobby and didn't see any For Rent sign, then, she saw a notice tacked above the mail boxes that read, "If you are interested in seeing the apartment that is for rent, please contact owner at phone number 957-3322. Erika thought it odd. Shouldn't there be someone there to take care of the showing and give her some information? After a moment's thought, she decided to press one of the buttons on one of the mail boxes. When she pressed it, the main door opened, and she entered quickly. As she entered, a lady came out of one of the apartments. She was just wearing a bathrobe and had curlers in her hair.

"Hello, can I help you?" the lady asked. "Oh yes," Erika replied. "Do you have any information on the apartment that is for rent?"

"Well I don't know what I can tell you. The man who owns it lived there for a short time and then moved away because he was transferred to Manhattan by his employer. His reason for requiring a prospect to call him to see the apartment is that he wants to see the one who is applying for it, in person and check them out. If you want to contact him and ask to see it, you may use my phone to call him." Erika readily accepted her offer and dialed the number.

"Mr. Burton's Office," a female voice answered.

"Yes I am interested in the apartment that is for rent. A note with this phone number to call was tacked up there," Erika stated.

"Oh, just a moment please, I will connect you to Mr. Burton."

In a couple of minutes a male voice came on and said, "I understand you are interested in the apartment I have for rent."

"Yes, my name is Erika Beiler, and I just arrived here from Pennsylvania and need to find a place to live." She paused a moment, but he didn't say anything, so she added quickly, "I really do need to find a place to live. I hope I can afford it as I like the area. It seems very clean compared to some I have looked at."

He paused again and then added, "Well, if you can wait there about forty-five minutes I will meet you and show it, and we can discuss the rent."

"I would appreciate that," she told him. Erika thanked the tenant for the use of her phone and introduced herself; then she started to leave.

The tenant said, "No problem at all. My name is Jody Grant, and I heard you say you just arrived from Pennsylvania.

I can tell you that some of these apartments are owned and some are rented, and some owners live in them and some rent them out. My husband and I rent this one, and we have been here five years, and we really like it here."

"I hope I can manage the rent." Erika said

"What kind of work do you do?" Jody asked.

"I came here to study to become a fashion designer," Erika said, and she went on to explain: "I have always dreamed of doing that and really like designing, and I also will need to find a job in the meantime. I come from an Amish family and an Amish community, and my parents didn't approve of me spending the time doing that. My father would always scold me and say, 'You are just wasting your time and dreams on that,' but I still have that desire."

"Oh I think that is wonderful." Jody said." If you take the apartment, we will try and help you as much as we can. I do work though, and this is my day off. "

"What type of work do you do?"Erika asked.

"I have a secretarial position for a legal firm in downtown Brooklyn," she answered.

"Gee," Erika said," I wish I knew that type of work. The only jobs that I have done were dressmaking and making decorated cakes for a bakery. I did that until I had enough money saved to come here. Now I will need to find something I can do to make a livelihood here."

"I'll keep my eyes open for anything that might help you." Jody said.

At that Erika thanked her for the use of her phone and concern and said, "I think I'll walk around outside until Mr. Burton arrives, and I hope to see you later, Jody."

She had just gotten outside when she noticed a bright red convertible car slowing up in front of the building. She watched to see if the driver would go up the steps to the entry. She saw he was headed in that direction, so she turned and headed back that way. As she approached him she asked, "Are you Mr. Burton, the gentleman I need to see about the apartment for rent."

"Are you Erika Beiler? I'm Rod Burton, and I think you want to see the apartment, right?"

"Yes, could I please just look at it?" she asked.

"Certainly, just follow me and we'll take a look."

She nodded and gave him a little smile. He is a very handsome man and courteous too, she thought to herself.

As they both started to ascend the stairs he turned and said to her, "You knew this was on the second floor and that it is furnished?"

"No, I didn't know. That might make the rent too expensive for me to afford." she replied.

He opened the door of the apartment and took her arm in a very gentle way to usher her in. She thought that was very nice. He was very good looking besides being courteous, she thought. He was tall and sharply dressed and looked very professional.

Erika's eyes widened at the sight she was seeing. She never dreamed that she would live in a home as lovely as this. The place was furnished and decorated in styles and designs she had only seen in magazines back home.

She followed as he pointed out the living / dining room that had a large window looking out at the park. All of the items in the room showed that they were chosen by someone with very fine taste. The room contained a lovely, small sofa; a lounge chair; coffee table; and two side tables holding exquisite lamps. Paintings on the walls were also of excellent taste. A small breakfast bar separated the kitchen from the living area. The kitchen was small but quite adequate. Then he directed her to the bedroom, which was not oversized but had room for a dresser, bed and a couple of lamp tables with lamps. The room repeated his good taste in design. Next to the bedroom was a bathroom with no tub but a shower. Next to that was a very large walk-in dressing room that contained a wardrobe with mirrors on the doors. The room also had a small window in it. She had never seen a closet that large before. She asked herself, will I ever have enough clothes to hang in there? Then she thought, she could use that for her work room and her drawings. That really delighted her.

"Perfect!" She blurted out

"What?" he asked.

"Oh I'm sorry. I was just thinking out loud that this room could be my work space for drawing. I know I won't need all that closet space for the few clothes I have."

"Are you an artist?" he asked.

"Well my goal is to become a fashion designer," she answered.

She went on to explain, "I came here to extend my education in that field and attend a school to broaden my knowledge. I know I will need to find a job in the meantime to be able to afford the schooling and the rent for this apartment—which you haven't told me what it is to be, as yet," she said questioningly.

"What kind of work are you looking for, and what happens if you don't find a job?" He asked.

She thought a minute and said, "I have got to find some income for living expenses and also be able to go to designers' school. I have money to hold me until I can find a job. I am a high school graduate but the only work I've done at home was selling my bakery goods and crafts at Amish fairs. Before I graduated, I designed and made custom gowns and clothing for the students at school for a few years, and after I graduated I took orders for making custom gowns and dresses and was commissioned to do more of it until my plans brought me here."

She had the feeling that he was very understanding and that she could confide in him. Again she thought he was very handsome, but that didn't seem to be the reason she felt close to him. She didn't quite know what it was. He was just her landlord, she told herself.

Neither of them spoke for a few minutes, then she asked him, "What rent are you asking for this apartment?" He studied her for a minute and smiled admiringly at her and said, "Well, I'll tell you, being that it is furnished, I was expecting to ask seven hundred a month, including utilities, and I wanted someone who would take good care of my furnishings." Hesitantly, he continued, "I am impressed with you and believe you will take good care of my place. I want to give you a break and help you get started here. Do you think you could manage four-fifty a month and still be able to afford your school costs?"

She jumped up and let out a squeal. "Oh! Thank you Mr. Burton," she replied with a big smile all over her face. She had the urge to embrace him and wanted to kiss him but decided to maintain her composure since she had just met him and he was her landlord.

"You may call me Rod," he said with a smile and his eyes sparkling.

Erika hurried to open her purse and pay him before he could change his mind. After she had given him the rent money and he started toward the door, he turned to her and said, "If you don't mind, I might come around occasionally to see how you are doing if that is agreeable with you."

"Oh! yes, by all means," she replied, as she hoped he would. "I really appreciate your consideration."

Bidding her goodbye, he walked down the hall towards the stairs and left.

As he reached the outside he began to think about the meeting he just had with his new tenant. She was a very pretty young lady and he was attracted to her humble appearance and her determination to reach her goal. He was confident she would make a good tenant. Noticing the demure way about her, he wondered if she could be strong enough to take the task of the drastic change from her life in the country to the life in this big city. She was alone in this big city, and he thought she may need someone to give her a little help. He gave her credit for the courage she showed. As he drove off, he decided that he would check on her occasionally to make sure she was alright until she was more accustomed to the change.

Moving away from the window, Erika's thoughts came back to the present time, she looked around the room again at the way it was furnished and couldn't believe her eyes at what she had now as a home. She made a decision that she would definitely make it now to fulfill her dream. This is where her dream has brought her, and she liked what she saw and the people she met so far. She thought about her landlord and how generous he seemed. He was also very handsome, and she surmised that he would be about twenty-six or twenty-seven years old and wondered if he was married. Did that make a difference to her? she asked herself.

Coming here and finding this apartment was a big step toward fulfilling her dream.

Then she realized she was so elated she wanted to tell someone her good news. Instantly, Jody, the lady downstairs, came to her mind. She was the only person she knew here. She couldn't call Darcy because she didn't have a phone as yet.

By that time it was getting evening time. She bolted down the stairs and knocked on the door of Jody's apartment.

In a few minutes the door opened and a nice looking man said, "Good evening, may I help you?"

"Oh, I'm so sorry, I hope I'm not disturbing you. I just wanted to see Jody. I hope she hasn't retired yet. I just took the apartment upstairs, and Jody was so gracious to me earlier today that I wanted to give her the good news."

"Oh, it's OK, Jody is still awake, come in."

As she entered, he said, "My name is Dan, and congratulations on your new find."

Jody entered the room, and Erika, all excited, repeated her good news to her. "Oh, I'm so happy for you, now you have a good start."

"Thank you, Jody, I'm sorry to disturb you and your husband at this late hour."

"That's OK, it's not too late for me, and Dan doesn't go in early tomorrow. He works for a large advertising firm, and he doesn't need to be there early every day," Jody explained.

"By the way, you have been so busy since you got here, have you had anything to eat?"

"As a matter of fact, I was going to ask you if there is a market close by that would be open at this time, and also, how do I go about getting the phone connected? "The instrument is there but it doesn't work," Erika told her.

"Well, there is a small market around the corner in the next block, and the phone company has an annex down that street also, but they may be closed. They will ask you a few questions, and they will probably require a deposit because you are from out of state and are not working yet. I can call and check to see if they are open for you if you like."

"Oh, that would be wonderful, thank you." Erika said.

Jody called, and they told her that they would be open for another thirty minutes.

Jody popped up and said, "I'll tell you what, we have some spaghetti and salad left over from our dinner and you are sure welcome to it, and you won't need to go to the market. You can go to the phone company and take care of that and pick up the spaghetti and salad on your way back. I know you must be tired and are anxious to lie down."

Erika accepted her offer and said she would definitely pick up the dinner that they offered her on her way back. Then she left.

Erika went to the phone company and took care of that, and they gave her a number and said it would be working in the morning. She went back to Jody's and picked up the spaghetti and salad, and after a little small talk, she thanked them and bid them goodnight. Carrying her dinner, she headed up to her apartment.

She was sure she would fall asleep as soon as her head hit the pillow, but she didn't. She kept thinking about what her next move would be. She knew she had to find a job, but doing what, she asked herself. And she thought of Darcy; she had to let her know she found an apartment and have Darcy let her parents know she was OK, since they didn't have a phone. She hoped she would have the phone working in the morning when she woke up. Those were things she would try to take care of right away. After getting all those things settled in her mind and being exhausted, she finally went to sleep.

Waking very early in the morning after looking around at her new apartment and being pleased with everything, her first thought was calling Darcy and letting her know she found a place and give her the address and phone number. She also wanted to ask her if she would please let her parents know and give them her new address. Darcy agreed to do that for her. Darcy told her she was ready to make a change, but she needed a few more dollars saved.

Erika's next important thought was finding a job. She decided to dress in something a little more appropriate to go out and find someplace to buy a newspaper and get some breakfast and search the want ads for a job.

After purchasing the newspapers, she found a coffee shop adjoining the apartment building and decided to have some coffee and donuts or something else to go with the coffee and sit there and scan the want ads. She walked in and found a table near a window where there would be plenty of light for reading. Reading the ads was a little difficult for her as she never before had to look at the want-ads for a job

As she continued searching, she had a feeling someone was staring in her direction. She looked up to see a very handsome man seated at a table across the aisle. As their eyes met, he offered her a broad smile, not knowing how to accept that, she returned a very shy, weak smile.

Returning her attention to her newspaper ads and scanning them carefully, she couldn't find anything that she imagined she would be suited for.

As she began to fold up the paper and started to finish her coffee and sweet roll, she felt a hand on her shoulder and looking up to see who it was. She looked straight into a pair of beautiful pale blue eyes that made her feel as though she was drowning in them. Her heart immediately did a flip-flop. It was the same man who had been sitting across the aisle from her. It startled her for a moment, then he said, "I'm sorry, I didn't mean to startle you, but I noticed you didn't seem to be from this area and it looked like you were searching for something in the newspaper and wondered if I could help you."

Not being familiar with someone approaching her like that, she didn't know what to do. So in a shy way she said, "Oh, that's alright, I was just looking for a job."

Then introducing himself he stated, "By the way, my name is Greg Watson, and I live at the Highmark Apartments just around the corner. What type of job are you searching for?"

Surprised at his first remark she replied, "I just rented an apartment in that building so I also live in those apartments. I was looking for some kind of work I thought I could do. My only experiences are ladies' fashions and sales."

"Well I hope you can find something you like because you seem like a very smart lady."

Surprised by his compliment she said, "Thank you," and began to gather up her papers.

"Would you like to meet me here for breakfast tomorrow morning? And in the meantime if I hear of anything I will think of you?"

She hesitated a moment, contemplating the invitation, then decided she would like that and accepted the offer. He thanked her and said he would look forward to it and left.

Erika gathered her papers and also left. She decided that on the way back to the apartment she would stop at the market and pick up a few grocery items for her larder so she would have something there to eat and not need to go out and buy her meals. All the while, she was thinking of Greg Watson. He seemed like a very nice gentleman, she thought. She had never had an experience like that when she lived on the farm or when she was going to high school. She had never been approached by the opposite sex in any manner. She always blamed that on her attire and mode of living

This encounter gave her a pleasant tingle through her body. Then, the idea came to her that she should try to improve her looks, maybe fix her hair, which had never been cut or styled. She had worn it in a bun since she left home. At home it was always up inside of her Amish bonnet. Perhaps a little lip color would help and maybe a little eye make-up. She had seen how the girls at the high school in Lancaster used it, and felt she could manage a little. So she made a small purchase of cosmetics.

After making her purchases, she headed in the direction of her apartment. On the way, as she looked around, she thought, how different everything was from where she came from. There is so much more activity here.

She wanted to stop and talk to Jody about her experience with Greg Watson, but she was certain she wouldn't be home from work at this early hour.

When she got into her apartment, she placed all the grocery items in their proper places, all the time she was doing that, she was thinking of the handsome man that she had breakfast with. And to think they both lived in the same apartment building. She couldn't wait until Jody came home to ask her about him. She was sure Jody would know something about him since he was one of the tenants there.

Being very anxious, she decided to put a note on Jody's door to call her as soon as she came home and left her new phone number she had gotten from the phone company, hoping it would work for Jody.

Soon the phone rang and she figured then, that it had been connected for her. She imagined that it would be Jody. She answered it.

"Hi, this is Jody. I got your note, what's up?"

"Oh Jody, I'm glad the phone number is working already. I wanted to tell you that I met this very nice man this morning in the coffee shop around the corner, and he introduced himself as Greg Watson and said he lived in this apartment building, and I thought I could ask you if perhaps you might know him and could tell me something about him."

Jody paused a moment, then replied, "Oh, yes, I know who he is. He lives down the hall from us in #110, and he seems like a nice guy, probably around 26 or 27 years old. We never had much association with him, but he did say he was in real estate. Why, did he ask you for a date?"

"No," Erika answered. "He said he would like me to meet him for breakfast tomorrow morning at the same coffee shop."

"I'm sure he would be fine to have breakfast with," Jody said.

"I'm glad you said that, Jody. Now all I need to do is improve my looks and do something with my hair and put some make-up on."

Jody laughed a little and said, "You won't need to do much, and if you need any help, just let me know, and I'll help you."

"Thank you Jody, I really appreciate all your help."

"That's OK you just go and have a nice pleasant breakfast." Jody told her.

When she got off the phone with Jody, she started to practice putting on the make-up she purchased and continued until she was satisfied. Then she went to her closet and searched for something to wear. She didn't have much to choose from. Her clothes were very limited, but she settled for a dark blue denim skirt, that she had made before she left home and a lilac soft knit top. That should look good with my hair coloring, she thought.

Her hair was blonde and silky and had a natural soft curl. It was very long and healthy looking (the Amish women did not believe in cutting their hair). She had been wearing it up in a bun in the back since she left home but decided that she would take it out of the bun and let it hang loose. It was slightly curly and it looked pretty hanging loose.

Erika had a difficult time falling asleep that night, between thinking about finding a job and also meeting with Greg Watson the next morning for breakfast. She was too excited to sleep.

When she awoke in the morning, the sun was shining brightly into her room. What a beautiful day, she thought as she peered out of her window and looked around. She wondered, since he hadn't set a time, what time Greg would be there, so she decided she would be there about the same time as the previous morning.

Excitedly, she showered and dressed and very carefully applied her new make-up.

Then it came time to plan how to wear her hair. She wanted it to be different, so her decision was to take her hair out of the bun and let it fall loose, making sure that every hair was in place. It looked very nice falling over her shoulders and down her back.

Arriving at the coffee shop at about the same time she went the day before, she looked around for a vacant table. Finding one near a window, she sat down. As she waited for service, she checked all the other tables and didn't see Greg. Wasn't he coming? Was this just a play of his? He might not have been serious—maybe he wasn't coming at all. Oh, well, that's life, she thought

She decided that she would go ahead and order anyway and looked over the menu for something not too expensive.

The waitress approached her table and asked, "Would you like coffee ma'am?"

"Yes, I'll take coffee, and I haven't decided what else I want."

Again checking the menu to find something light, she felt a gentle hand on her shoulder and as she looked up, she peered directly into those pale, blue eyes.

"Good morning," he greeted her. "I'm glad you didn't forget. May I join you?"

She motioned for him to take a seat.

"You look very lovely on this beautiful, morning," he said as he motioned for the waitress and ordered her to bring him coffee.

"Have you ordered?" He asked Erika.

"No, I haven't. I was just checking for something light," she replied. Looking at the waitress, she ordered a bowl of fruit and toast. He ordered scrambled eggs and bacon.

As the waitress departed, he said to her, "Have you located a job yet?"

"No, not yet, I've been busy getting settled and having a phone installed."

"Well, I'm sure you will," he assured her. "As I said yesterday, I will keep my eyes and ears open. I know there is something out there for you."

With a questioning look, she asked, "Why, do you say that, have you heard of something?"

"No, but you are a very attractive young lady, and I don't think you'll have too much trouble finding something. Do you definitely have fashion designing as your goal?"

"Yes, that's what I have always aimed for since I was a little girl"

He looked at her with a kind smile and asked, "Do you have any drawings to show with your resume?"

"No," she replied. "I'm still working on some, and they are still on my drawing board. I was thinking, perhaps I would look for another type of job to do until I was more prepared."

"I think that is a very good idea," he said, agreeing with her. "Tell me about you," he asked. "Where you are from and what did you do before you came here." Erika took another bite of her toast and a sip of her coffee as Greg dug into his scrambled eggs.

Then she began to tell him the story of where she was from and a little about her Amish childhood and going to a different high school and how she was determined to hold to her dream to become a fashion designer.

Greg seemed fascinated with her story, and when she stopped, he just looked at her admiringly and didn't say anything for a minute.

Bringing him back to their conversation, she said, "Now, tell me about you. How long have you lived here, and how long have you been in real estate?"

He said he was from Maryland and was in insurance sales there but wanted to better himself, so he came to New York four years ago and became a real estate broker and was now doing much better.

In their conversation, he also told her that he had been seeing a lady friend for about a year, and then a couple of months ago, they decided to sever their relationship. He didn't reveal a reason for doing that.

He asked her if she had a steady boyfriend and she said, "No, I have never had any associations with the opposite sex. My people frowned on that unless we were serious about marriage and children." She explained that she had not been ready for that as she wasn't ready for anything to interfere with her designing plans.

He sat there studying her face as she spoke and said, "I hope you don't always feel that way," and smiled at her.

After she asked him more about New York, and there was a little more small talk, he said he would need to get to work. Then he said to her, "I would like to see you again. If you agree to give me your telephone number, I will call you."

She agreed, and he jotted it down. After saying he would call her, he got up, gave her a loving squeeze, picked up both meal tabs, and paid the waitress and left.

Rising from her seat to look out of the window, she could see him getting into a big shiny black car.

She was still bewildered by the attention he had given her. She was very attracted to him and liked him, but felt she would like to know more about him.

Purchasing more newspapers to scour the ads and see if she could find something, she went back to her apartment to read them over. She didn't find anything that suited her. Then she saw an advertisement of an employment agency which seemed to interest her.

She called the phone number on the ad and the girl answering said, "Alert Employment Service, may I help you?"

Erika replied, "Yes, I'm looking for a job, and I noticed your ad in the paper and thought you might be able to help me."

"What sort of position are you looking for?" the girl asked.

"What do you have available? Erika asked

"Well, we have various jobs open, but I think it would be best if you came in for an interview," the girl replied.

After obtaining the address from the girl and setting up an appointment for the next day, she ended the call.

Later she decided she would sit down at her drawings and see what she could do. After trying and not being satisfied with anything she was doing, she decided she just wasn't in the mood as she was thinking too much about her breakfast with Greg. This was the first man that had ever shown interest in her and that pleased her very much.

She began to think about her own wardrobe and how sparse it was. She really needed some new clothes, and since she was a designer, why didn't she design some things for her own use? She was very happy she had brought her sewing machine with her. It was an old one operated by a foot treadle, but it still worked fine.

So she decided she was going to make a few new things for her wardrobe, and tomorrow when she went to the employment agency, she would look for a place to purchase her fabric and the necessary sewing items. Then she sat down at the drawing board and started to design some things that she would like. When she finished drawing something she was satisfied with, she had a very good idea what kind of material she wanted, and decided she would look for that. She spent most of that day working on designing her own wardrobe.

As she was preparing a snack before retiring, the phone rang, and it was Jody.

"Hi, how did your breakfast go, this morning?" she asked

"Oh, it was very nice, and he was a perfect gentleman, and he asked if he could see me again and if I would give him my phone number."

"Did you?" Jody asked.

"Yes." Erika said.

"Do you like him?" Jody asked.

"Well, I think he is very nice, and I would like very much to know him better. He seems very gentle and his pale blue eyes just want me to drown in them when I look at him."

"Ho, Ho, Ho, I guess you do like him if he does that to you," she laughed.

"Well, we'll see if I ever see him again." Erika said.

"By the way, I have an appointment with an employment agent tomorrow, and I hope I can get something," She told Jody.

"I'll keep my fingers crossed for you," Jody told her.

"Thank you. Good night Jody," she said and hung up.

The next day she traveled to town and found the address of the employment agency that she had talked to on the phone. She opened the door hesitantly, went in and saw the receptionist and three other ladies waiting to be helped.

She went to the receptionist's desk and said, "I made an appointment yesterday for a consultation with someone here."

"What is your name?" the receptionist asked

"Erika Beiler." Erika answered.

"Please have a seat and we will call you when a consultant is available."

In a few minutes the receptionist called her name and she was ushered into a very small office.

Soon a short, stout man entered. "I am Mr. Brooks. What type of a position are you looking for, young lady?" he asked.

"Well, I prefer something that is associated with fashion designing, but I will take anything that I am capable of doing because I really need a job right now."

"What kind of experience do you have in fashion designing?" he asked

"Mr. Brooks, I just came here from Pennsylvania to pursue an education in the fashion designing field. I have done a lot of it just on my own back home, but I have a desire to further my knowledge in that direction. In the meantime, I need a livelihood until I can enter a fashion institute."

After a slight pause, he asked, "What other experience do you have?"

"I have been an assistant to a dressmaker and have done some sales work," She answered.

It seemed as though he was thinking and then he said. "I'll tell you what ... Erika Beiler is it?"

"Yes" she said.

"You leave your name and phone number with the receptionist, and I will give you a call if we find something for you," he advised her.

Erika did that, then left the office. She didn't feel very encouraged with the meeting with him, but she felt she just had to wait and see if he would call her.

Her next project was making some new clothes for herself. So she located a fabric store and found just the type of material she wanted. Then she headed for her apartment to begin making her own new apparel. She worked on that for the next week, and when she finished, she was extremely pleased that she had three very smart looking outfits. She knew she would need to work on more of them as soon as she could.

She hadn't heard from Greg Watson in that time, so she thought he had forgotten all about her, but she didn't mind as she had been busy with her sewing.

Displaying her new apparel to Jody that she had made, Jody's opinion was that she had done a very outstanding job, and they were so different from what she could have found in any store. One was a very pretty, light wool dress in a light, beige color. It had a contrasting trim around the "V" neckline with a flap on one side that folded back over a sleeveless jacket having a plaid pattern in the beige and brown colors that coordinate with the dress. It looked very chic on her. Another was a simple dress with a square neckline, and it also had a flap type collar that folded back and a below-the-knee length. It was in a navy blue linen material with white collar and cuffs. Then the next one was a circular skirt in a very nice shade of brown and a top to go with it in brown and gold patterned polyester with a scarf neck line that flipped over one side of the shoulder and down the back.

She was very pleased with them and knew she needed to make more as soon as she could afford the material.

She hadn't heard anything from the employment agency as yet, but surely they could find her something, she thought.

A few days later, she did get a call from Darcy and she told her that she was ready to come to New York and did she have a place for her to stay? She told Erika she had contacted her folks and they were happy to hear that she was OK and that they were getting along alright

Erika told Darcy that she could stay with her if she liked, and that she had a small room which could be arranged as her room. So Darcy said she would contact Erika as soon as she was going to leave and come there.

Immediately after hanging up the phone from Darcy, there came a knock at the door. "Who could that be? She thought. "Oh, it might be Greg. She hadn't heard from him for more than a week." She hoped that she looked presentable, and she glanced in the mirror as she walked by and pushed the strands of hair out of her face.

Opening the door she was shocked, because instead of Greg it was Rod Burton. This is a very pleasant surprise, she thought to herself.

"I'm sorry, I should have called first," he said. "I was in the neighborhood on a business call and thinking of you, I just decided to drop by. You did tell me it would be alright?" He asked, trying to excuse his boldness. He really wanted to see her again but was being somewhat coy about it.

"That's alright, won't you come in?" she asked as he walked into the living room.

"Won't you have a seat? I'm sorry I don't look very presentable, but I wasn't expecting anyone" she said, excusing her appearance.

She was thinking, it wasn't very nice—he really should have called first—but it did give her a little thrill that he was thinking about her.

"Oh you look fine. I just wanted to check to see if you needed anything and if you were OK. I also thought as long as I had to be in this area, I would drop off your rent receipt. I didn't give you one when you paid me."

"Thank You," she said as she accepted it from him.

"So, is everything going all right with you? Have you found employment yet? Or have you enrolled in a design school?" he asked.

"Everything is fine with the apartment, I'm really happy here. No, I haven't found employment yet, but I am working with an agency and they are trying to find something for me; and no, I haven't started a school yet either, I thought I had better concentrate on a job first, that seems to be a priority right now."

"Well, I hope you will soon find something that you will be happy with, and I look forward to you being my tenant here for a very long time," he told her. Wasn't that so sweet of him, she thought to herself.

"Oh I hope I do find something soon." she said.

Then she said to him, "By the way, a friend of mine from Pennsylvania is coming to see me and I was thinking that I might have her stay here with me for awhile. Would you object to that?" she asked. He thought about that for a minute then answered, "No, if you think you can manage that, I think I can."

"Oh thank you" she said

"Have you ever been to New York before?" he asked.

"No, this is the first time."

"Well then, I don't suppose you have seen much of New York since you have been here, have you?"

"No, I have only been around here and in downtown Brooklyn to see the employment agent," she answered.

"Well, I would like to show you some of New York, if you will allow me. I was thinking of taking you to dinner and a Broadway show some evening if you think you would like that. I could pick you up, and we would go to dinner, and later we could see the show."

Feeling elated, she accepted his offer. "That would be wonderful. I have never seen a stage show," she said.

"If you have a phone now, could I have the number and I will call as soon as I get the tickets and let you know the night it will be, if that is alright with you.

"Oh yes, I have." she answered. "I'll give you the number," she said as she jotted it down for him.

"Have you been working on your drawing?' he asked

"Yes, I keep up with that as much as I can," she replied.

"That's nice to hear. I must be going now. I'll call and let you know the date, and I'll see you later," and he put his arm on her shoulder and gave her a little squeeze.

Erika opened the door for his exit and said, "Goodnight."

After he left, Erika wondered about his visit. Did he really come to give her the rent receipt or was it for another reason? Anyway, she thought it was very nice of him to invite her to dinner and a show. Besides that she thought he was a very handsome man. He had dark, slightly curly hair and dark eyes and a very smooth shaven complexion, and both times she had seen him he looked like he just stepped out of a male fashion magazine, neatly dressed.

The following week, she was working with her drawings and she received a phone call.

"Hi, Erika, it's Darcy. I'm catching the bus, and I should be there in the morning," she blurted out in an excited voice.

"Great! Do you think you can find the address?"Erika asked.

"Oh yes, I'll take a cab, and the driver will know where it is."

"OK, but give me a call before you take the cab, OK?"

"Yes, I will, see you in the morning," Darcy told her

"Well, you be careful. There are a lot of military men around, and you don't know just who to trust." Erika warned her.

"Oh, don't worry, I'll be alright," Darcy said.

Erika rose very early in the morning and looking around the apartment she decided to start to plan on how she was going arrange her extra room for Darcy. She guessed she would move her drawing equipment into her bedroom or maybe in the living room. They would also need to find another bed for Darcy.

After getting things arranged in her mind as to how they could arrange things, it seemed to go alright for Erika and she thought she would wait until Darcy came to see if she had any ideas. The rest would work out alright, as they could share a lot of things. She was so happy Darcy was coming because she wouldn't feel so alone now.

Later that day, she received the call from Darcy saying that she had arrived in New York and was taking the cab and should be there soon. Close to the time that she expected Darcy, Erika sat at the window where she could see the cab when it arrived.

Soon she saw the cab pull up at the curb, and Darcy alighted with her luggage. To help her with her luggage and direct her to the apartment, Erika went down to greet her. As she was welcoming her, Jody came out to welcome her and help with the luggage. Erika introduced Darcy to Jody and told her that she was going to be staying with her and she would probably be seeing her around

After all the welcoming and hugging and all loaded down with the luggage, they made it to the apartment. Jody wished Darcy a pleasant stay and then bid them both a good afternoon and departed.

Darcy said she thought Jody was very nice and friendly and told Erika she thought the apartment was darling and so happy it had the extra room for her. Together they discussed getting it comfortable for her and how they would share the expenses and what they were going to do about their work to earn money.

After she was there a few days Darcy went out and purchased a bed for her room. Until she did that, she had been sleeping on the sofa in the living room. Things were going along really good since she came, and both were content now.

Every day, Darcy would go out and check to find some kind of work. When she had been there about a week, she found a job at Bloomingdales in the linen department as a sales clerk. She was real happy about having wages coming in, and Erika was real happy for her also.

Chapter 2
FINDING EMPLOYMENT

Erika hadn't found any type of work yet and hadn't heard anything from the employment agent either. Darcy suggested she try Bloomingdales; she was pretty sure she could get something there. Erika had gotten to the point where she was really considering that.

About the time she was going to go to Bloomingdales and try that, she received a call from the employment agent, asking her if she could come in for a consultation because he thought he had found just the right position for her.

"I think I have found something that will suit you," Mr. Brooks told her. So she made an appointment for the following day, and she became very excited and hoped that it would be something she could do.

When she met with him the next day, he told her he really believed that he found something that she might like. He said, "I have a well-known fashion designer looking for an assistant with a background in designing who could take intricate instructions."

He said he was sure she would be very satisfied with the salary that he was offering, but he didn't say what it would be. Erika was to see the designer the very next day.

He gave her the address and forms she was to have the new employer sign, if she obtained the position. He said his fee for his services would be ten percent of her first month's salary. At first that sounded like a lot, but then she thought it would depend on what her salary would be.

She didn't waste any time making the meeting for the new job the very next day. She had a little difficulty finding the place because it was in downtown Manhattan. Finally she did find it. It was in a very modern building with a large lobby decorated in exceptionally very fine taste. Once again, she was impressed at the décor especially for an office building.

There was a receptionist sitting at the desk, and Erika handed her the card and asked if she could be directed to that office. The receptionist complied, pointing in the direction of the office.

Finding the office, she noticed the name on the door in gold which said, "Designs by IAN." She walked in and found herself amid three desks and several large work tables and a few manikins standing around and many, many bolts of different kinds of fabrics. Some were so beautiful like she had never seen before. There was a man at one of the tables, and it looked like he was cutting some fabrics, and an older-looking lady sitting at one of the two sewing machines. They both acknowledged her entrance and asked her to please have a seat and someone would be with her shortly.

As she sat there waiting for the man she was to see, she began to think about her appearance and wondered what his impression would be of her. She wasn't dressed as one would expect a designer to be dressed. If he would just give her a chance to afford to improve her appearance she knew she could do it.

Soon a gentleman came swaggering into the room, almost like he was entering a stage with sort of a feminine walk. He was a small man in stature and partly bald, and he seemed very pleasant.

"Hi there, I guess you are the young lady that the employment agency sent. "Erika Byler is it?"

"Yes, but we pronounce it Beeler and it is spelled Beiler," she answered.

"My name is Ian Graham. I'm the designer here, and that gentleman over there is Roger, my cutter and assistant when I need one, and over there is Betsy my seamstress." He pointed towards them waving his open hands. "Please have a seat and you can tell me what kind of experience you have had in this field."

"Yes, thank you," she said, as she took a seat at one of the large work tables and went into all the details of her life and her desire to pursue a designing career before she came to New York.

Then he said, "I would like to see some of your designs. Do you have a portfolio of your work?"

"Yes," she said, "I also have photos of some of the things I was commissioned to do and I will be happy to bring them in and show you."

So he asked her if she could have them there the next day. She said, "Yes, of course." He then set a time for her to meet him, and after agreeing with that she left

After she left the office, she began thinking about him. Was she going to be happy working for him? She asked herself. He seemed very nice and a perfect gentleman, but his gestures were so feminine, almost lady-like. She wasn't familiar with that.

When she got home, she thought she would tell Darcy about her meeting and about her concern with this employer and his odd gestures.

Darcy said to her, "Maybe he is gay."

Erika looked at her bewildered and asked, "What's that?"

So Darcy tried to explain to her that he will not be physically attracted to her because he would only be attracted to other men.

"Maybe I won't be happy working with that type of person," she said to Darcy.

"Oh, don't worry about that. Those particular men are harmless to women, and if you are nice to them, you will be their friend. I am sure you will be fine with him."

"Oh really" she asked.

"Yes, and he'll probably treat you as just another loyal worker like himself." That seemed to ease her fears, and she became more enthused.

She gathered up all of her drawings and her portfolio and whatever photos she had of her work and planned to see him the next morning.

When she arrived at the studio the next morning, Ian was seated at the large work table waiting for her. She spread out her work and while Ian was in deep concentration looking over her work and rubbing his chin, she wondered what he was thinking.

Finally he looked up at her and said, "You have done some fabulous work here and to think you did all of this without any formal schooling. The only criticism I have is that most of the fabrics are not the best, but I understand you must have had a hard time getting the fabrics you wanted and didn't have access for fine fabrics—as I do here in New York," he said.

Then he said to her, "Erika I'll tell you what—I would like you to join my firm, and you will have the opportunity and materials to better yourself, and you will learn as you go, and you will have no need to enroll in a school."

He told her what the salary would be plus there would be the chance of advancement. Erika was flabbergasted and didn't waste any time to accept his offer. She couldn't believe her ears.

She could hardly wait to spread the news to Darcy, Jody and even Greg and Rod, when she had the opportunity to see them again

She hadn't seen Greg since their breakfast together. Then she wondered why. It was about four weeks or more since then, and he did say he was going to call her.

When she returned home, Darcy was home from work already, which was too early for her to be home. Erika was sort of surprised and wondered why.

"What's up Darcy?"Erika asked.

"Oh, I got booted today"

"What do you mean booted, I don't understand?"

"Well I was late clocking in on three different days, so they laid me off."

"Oh, I'm so sorry." Erika said.

"Don't worry, I'll find another job, probably something I will like better. I wasn't real happy there."

Erika, feeling overwhelmed with excitement, blurted out with her great news before she even sat down. She told Darcy all about the studio and all that Ian said about her work. Darcy was very happy for Erika, but Erika was very sad that Darcy had lost her job. She felt sure Darcy would find something else because she did have experience in sales.

They both sat there and talked over all the recent happenings of their employment events.

Then Erika felt that she wanted to retired very early that night as it was a fruitful day for her, and she was tired. As she lay there, she started to think about Greg. Why hadn't she heard from him? Was there something wrong? Was he disenchanted with her already; and what about Rod Burton? He was going to call her when he was able to get the theatre tickets, but she hadn't heard from him for nearly three weeks also. Oh well, perhaps he has a lady friend that is taking up his time. I guess I won't lose any sleep over them, she thought, and finally dozed off to sleep.

The next morning Erika saw Darcy before she left for work and Darcy told her that this day she was going to see the employment agent that Erika went to and see if he could find something for her. She was getting desperate to find something now.

When Erika got to her studio that morning, Ian was there, and he told her he was going to give her a couple of his commissioned jobs to work on to see what she could do with them, and if she did a good job, he would have her join him in his big designers' fashion show that he had planned to put on later in the year. He was very impressed with the way that she incorporated the special outstanding touches that very few designers would think of. He told her that he was also planning on going to France and Italy to find some exquisite fabrics to use for the fashion show. That made Erika delighted and anxious to get started on the jobs he was giving her.

When she got home, she had more good news to tell Darcy, about her boss giving her some of his commission orders to work on. Darcy said she was very proud of her.

Then Darcy told her about her meeting with Mr. Brook, the employment agent. She said he questioned her about her experience. During his talk with her, he told her that he noticed that she had very pretty hands and slender fingers and seemed to know how to use them. That gave him an idea. He said maybe he could find something in the modeling / sales field for her, perhaps in jewelry. He was going to try that avenue and see if he could locate something in that field. She was pleased with that and thought she would probably like that.

As Erika and Darcy were talking, the phone rang and Darcy answered it. Turning to Erika, she said handing her the phone. "It's for you, some man."

Erika took the phone and said, "This is Erika."

"Hi there, this is Greg and how have you been? I haven't talked to you for awhile, how are you doing? Have you found anything yet?"

"Oh hi Greg, I am fine, and yes, I am working with a designer in Manhattan, and I really like it. He is sure that I will learn enough with him that I won't require any other schooling."

"Great! I knew you would find something you would like. By the way, do you have Saturday free?" he asked.

"Yes, I don't work weekends unless I want to, why do you ask?"

"Well, I need to go out to the Bay area and check out some property Saturday, and I thought you might enjoy the drive out there. We could have lunch there. What do you say?"

"That sounds very nice, Greg. What time shall I be ready?"

After giving her the time and telling her that he would be at her door at that time, the call was completed.

She began to think about what she would wear. Oh, yes, she would wear one of her new dresses she made, probably the navy blue with the white trim.

She had a very hard time going to sleep that night, thinking of Greg and their date.

It must have been about three o'clock in the morning and Erika awoke with a very loud knocking on the front door. She jump out of bed and bumped into Darcy coming out of her room; she was awakened also.

"What is that?" Darcy asked.

"It sounds like someone at our door," was Erika's answer.

When they both got to the door together Darcy warned her, "Well don't you open that door until you know who is out there."

So Erika yelled out, "Who is there?"

And the answer was, "It's Dan, from down stairs Erika, can I talk to you?"

"Who's Dan?" Darcy asked

"He's Jody's husband, and they live downstairs," she said as she opened the door.

"What's wrong, Dan?" she asked after she had opened the door.

"Have you seen Jody? I can't find her, and she hasn't been home from work, and that is not like her."

"No I haven't, Dan. I stopped by after work and wanted to tell her my good news, and she wasn't home then. Oh, by the way, this is my friend from Pennsylvania. Darcy this is my neighbor, Dan," she said introducing them.

"Where have you looked for her? Does she ever go shopping after she gets off work?" Erika asked.

"When she does she always informs me first," was his answer.

"I have checked with all of her friends, and I went by her office where she works, and they say she left at her regular time. I couldn't see her car where she usually parks it either." He told them.

"Is there any place that we can go to look for her?" Darcy asked.

"I'm afraid not. Neither of you are familiar with this area; I'm sure you would both get lost, but thank you anyway," he replied.

"Did you notify the police?" Darcy asked.

"Yes, and they said she would need to be missing another day before they could treat it as a missing person case."

"I certainly would keep after the police and see if there isn't something that they could possibly do to help you find her." Darcy said.

"Well I'm going down there to talk to them again and see what they have to say," he told them.

"If you find out anything, please let us know, and let us know what the police have to say," Erika told him. "What did they say when you first saw them?" she asked.

"Just that she must be gone another day before it is a missing person case for them to look for her."

They all thought that was terrible. It seems that there would be something the police could do. With a beaten look on his face, he turned and walked away toward the stairs.

After Dan left, they both decided they wouldn't sleep anyway and might just as well put on some coffee and talk.

While they were having their coffee, Darcy asked Erika if Jody and Dan were happy together and Erika said, as far as she could see, they were very much in love and very compatible.

But where could Jody be was the question? Did Jody and Dan have a quarrel and Jody didn't want to come home to him. Erika said that she had never heard them say a nasty word to each other since she met them. Could Jody have just gone away from Dan? Did she find someone new and ran away with him? Erika said she couldn't picture that, they seemed to be very much in love. Hopefully they would know something more tomorrow.

Then the conversation went to Greg Watson, and Erika told Darcy how she had met him and all about his pale blue eyes and how they affected her. She also told her about Rod Burton and how she felt about him and he was going to take her to dinner and a show, but she hadn't heard from him for several weeks. She knew that he was a busy man who probably had someone to occupy his social time with.

She said she liked both of these men and Darcy said laughing, "Wow! Erika, it sounds like you may have a battle on your hands if you aren't careful."

Then Erika said, "Well, they are both very nice and both gentlemen, and I don't know either of them very well, so how can I make a decision?

And why do I need to make a decision right now? I want to get to know more about Rod first." Darcy agreed to that.

It was Friday today, and on her way to work, Erika was thinking about her date with Greg tomorrow. She wondered what it was like out by the bay. Would she see the ocean? She had never seen a large amount of water like that, and the thought of it made her excited. And every time she thought of how nice Greg was, her body tingled again. She couldn't wait to see him. Would he think she looked pretty in her new dress? She could hardly wait for tomorrow to get there.

When she arrived at the studio, Ian was there, seated at one of the large tables talking to Roger, his cutter. It seemed to Erika that they had been in a very heated conversation. The minute that Erika appeared, Roger got up and left.

Ian asked Erika to please come into his office with him. When she came in he said, "Sit down, Erika, I want to give you some instructions about the two commissioned jobs that I'm going to turn over to you."

Erika found her seat and waited for him to speak.

"I have this one lady who wants something very outstanding to wear at a televised federal political benefit, and it must be very attractive and chic. I will give you her dimensions and coloring, and I will select the fabric for you. The other one is for a very prominent lady, and she requires something that is extremely dressy for a formal installation benefit. I will also give you her dimensions and coloring and select the gorgeous fabric for that one also. I expect the very best for both of these ladies. They are very important clients of mine."

"Do you think you can do this?" he asked. "If you think you can, I will turn them over to you, and if you do well, I will have you join me in my fashion show that I have coming up later in the year." He had repeatedly offered that to her previously.

Erika assured him that she could do as he asked.

After her meeting with Ian, she went to her drawing board and started on some ideas for those important jobs. Later, he came to her and gave her more instructions for the jobs and the samples of the fabrics she was to use. He also critiqued her work a little, and told her to keep up the good work, then she returned to her drawing.

She wanted to get started on them today because tomorrow was her day off, and she had promised to see Greg that day. She worked on her drawings for the balance of that day.

As she was leaving the studio, she passed Ian's office and she could hear him and Roger arguing again in there. She guessed that Ian was unhappy about Roger's work, but she just ignored it and continued on her way.

When she left the studio and was on her way home, she wondered if Dan had located Jody yet. I will stop and check with him and see if he has found out anything about her, she decided.

As she approached her apartment building, she saw several police cars in front with their lights flashing. Oh gosh! She thought. I hope it's nothing bad about Jody. I hope they found her and that she is OK. As she got to Jody's apartment door, which was standing open, she saw several policemen in there talking to Dan. He was sitting down with his head in his hands. He looked up and saw Erika and asked her to come on in. "What is happening, Dan?" she asked.

"They found Jody," he said in a very dejected way.

"Is she alright?" she asked

"No, she is pretty well beaten up, and she is in the hospital right now."

"What in the world happened? Will she be alright?" she asked

"She was unconscious when they found her, but she has come out of it now and they think she will be OK," he said as he went on to explain somewhat about what happened. He said that he didn't have all of the details yet.

"They found her car near a building and then started looking for her and finally found her under some stairs of a building close to the one where she works. It seems someone hit her on the head with something heavy and knocked her out and beat her up viciously, then raped her. Because she was trying to fight them off, she was beaten up pretty bad. Thinking she was dead, they thought they would hide her under the stairs and then they beat it. The police are investigating everything now."

"Oh, Dan, that's terrible. I am so sorry. I wish there was something I could do. I will try to go to see her as soon as I can, when she can have visitors."

"Thank you, Erika, I really appreciate that," he said.

Seeing he was very busy with the law and with a sympathetic gesture, she squeezed his hand and said, "Please let me know if you discover anything, will you, Dan?" Then she bid him goodnight and went up the stairs to her apartment. She planned on talking to Dan and getting more details about Jody tomorrow.

When she got to her apartment, Darcy was there ahead of her and was all excited. She told Erika that the employment agent thought that he had a position for her to inquire about tomorrow. Erika asked her to tell her about it. She said it was a sales clerk in a very high-class jewelry store, and she would be on commission plus a low wage, and there was a chance for increases. But she wasn't sure that she was going to be happy with that.

"Well that sounds pretty good, what is your worry?" Erika asked her.

"I have never sold jewelry, and I don't know very much about it as I've never had much fine jewelry myself," she explained,

"Will they give you a chance to learn about it?" Erika asked. "Oh yes, they will allow me thirty days to get the hang of it," she answered.

"Well, that's not bad, but I know what you mean, I've never had any jewelry at all, and I wouldn't know anything about selling it either. But you know what? I better learn something about it also, so I know how to accessorize the gowns and outfits with it after I design them, and maybe you will be able to guide me with that. Do you think?"

Darcy agreed with her, and Erika said, "Go for it, Darcy, you may get to like it a lot and with the presentations you can give them with your lovely hands you may just end up making a lot of money."

That brought a big smile on Darcy's face, and she said, "I think I will take it if they want to hire me."

They talked a little about Jody and Erika related what Dan had told her regarding the situation and said she would try and see Dan tomorrow before she left with Greg and find out more details about the mystery.

Speaking of Greg made Erika more excited. What is with me, getting so excited as soon as he comes to my mind? She thought to herself. She didn't find herself feeling that way when she thought of Rod Burton. Thinking of Rod, why hadn't she heard from him? It had been more than two weeks since he came to see her. Oh well, maybe he changed his mind

After they had a small dinner and talked awhile, she and Darcy decided they would call it a day. Both walked into their bedrooms, and just as Erika started to remove her dress, there was a knock on the front door.

Gosh! Who in the world can that be? She asked herself as she went to the door. Remembering Darcy's warning, she called out, "Who is there?"

The answer came back. "It's Dan, Erika I didn't have much time to talk to you earlier," he said as Erika opened the door to let him in.

"I wanted to tell you all that happened, but with the cops there, I didn't have time."

"Oh, that's OK, I understand. What did really happen?" She asked.

"Well, all we could get out of Jody was this—it seems that these two guys jumped her as she was getting into her car at her parking space and forced her back in her car and took her out someplace, she didn't know where it was. She said it seemed like it was by a railroad track and when they tried to rape her, she tried to fight them off, so they began to beat her up, and then they knocked her out by hitting her on the head with something big—they don't know yet what they used to do that. Because she was fighting them off, they beat her until she was unconscious so she couldn't resist. Then according to the hospital, they both violated her badly in all ways. They put her back in her car, and by that time they thought that she was dead and probably didn't remember what building it was where they had picked her up. So, they took her to the wrong building and dumped her under those stairs and left. Thank God she was still alive."

"Oh My God" Erika blurted out "I have never heard of anything so horrible," "Have they caught the men?"

"Not yet, but they are working on some leads. If I ever get my hands on those bastards I'll kill them," Dan said.

"Poor Jody, I hope she can get well real soon and get this off her mind. I miss her," Erika said with tears in her eyes."If there is anything that Darcy or I can do, please, let us know."

"Thank you again. I appreciate that, and I know Jody will also," he said as he went out the door.

"What a nice man," Darcy said to Erika."What a terrible thing to happen to such a nice person."

After that unhappy interruption, they both continued to disrobe and climb into their beds.

Erika wanted to be fresh for Greg tomorrow.

Just as she got into bed and covered up, the phone rang. Now who could that be? She got up and grabbed the phone and said, "Hello?"

"It's only nine o'clock so I was hoping I wasn't going to catch you in bed. I didn't, did I?"

It was Rod Burton. Recognizing his voice, she answered, "Well, almost. I had just crawled in."

"Oh, I'm sorry to disturb you. I wanted to tell you that I finally acquired the tickets to the stage show called *Oklahoma*. Have you seen it?"

"No, remember, I told you I had never seen a stage show before."

"Well, this is slated to be one of the best, and the tickets are for Wednesday. Are you free that night?"

"Yes, I can be, Rod," she answered feeling a little thrill run down to her toes.

"Then I will pick you up about six o'clock, and we can have dinner around seven and then see the show after dinner, OK?"

"That sounds fine with me," she agreed.

After she hung up she started to laugh out loud.

Darcy asked "What in the world are you laughing at?"

"It just struck me funny that this evening has been one person after another on the phone or in this apartment all evening."

She had to tell Darcy what Rod Burton said before she went back to bed. Darcy said that she heard the conversation and was glad he had finally called her with the news that she was waiting to hear.

Now she had two dates to prepare for. Which one was she going to like the best? Then she thought she had better not think about the men too much. She should concentrate on her career because that was her goal. She was getting a good feeling from the attention of these men. It was something she had never experienced before. She went to sleep thinking of her situation and about tomorrow.

She awoke very early and felt a little groggy from thinking about all that had been happening. Today was a big day for her, and she started to plan on getting ready to see Greg. There she goes again—thinking of him makes her tingle all over. He had told her that he would call before he came to pick her up, so she was going to wait for his call. In the meantime, she showered and picked out the things that she was going to wear. As she stepped out of the shower, the phone rang and she answered it and it was Greg. He said he would come to her door in about one hour and was that OK. She said, "Yes, I will be ready."

She hurried to dress and put on her make-up, combed her hair and decided she would let it hang loose for a change she had been wearing it in a bun. She had planned to wear her navy blue dress with white trim that she had just made for herself.

It wasn't long until he knocked on her door, and after a goodbye to Darcy, she opened the door and greeted him. He took her arm and ushered her down to his car, which was parked down in the underground garage. She was ready to go.

As he drove on, he turned to her and said, "You look very lovely this morning, as usual."

"Thank you, it's really a lovely morning isn't it?" she said.

"Yes it is, and I believe you will enjoy this ride today. You will get to see more of Brooklyn and some of Manhattan. Perhaps we can view the Statue of Liberty and Ellis Island. Would you like that?"

"Yes," she answered. "I haven't seen much of New York since I've been here, and it's nice to be out and look things over and very nice of you to offer me this outing."

"Oh, no, it's my pleasure because I wanted to see you again."

Erika looked over at him and smiled. They talked about his work and what some of the people requested and how he would need to search to satisfy their wants.

They also talked about Erika and her desires and how she liked the job she had now. Then he asked her what her future plans would be.

"I hope that I can make it to the top as a designer—that's what I aimed for," she said.

"Well, I give you credit, and I also hope you do that," he said.

After he looked at the building that he came there to check on, they did see the Statue of Liberty, and then he stopped at a nice little café near the water, and they had lunch. All during lunch he was looking at her with those beautiful pale blue eyes, and she was melting. When they rose to leave he squeezed her around the waist. She was beginning to like his every touch.

When they had finished their lunch, they just walked along the waterfront, and Erika got to see the bay and a few sailboats out there on the water. Greg explained about the sailboats and she listened intently. She had never seen them before. Then they headed back to the car.

As he started to drive off, he reached over and pulled her closer to him and put his arm around her shoulder, she could feel his warm body while he was driving. Feeling his body so close to her made her body tingle again.

Then she told him of the tragedy with Jody and how she was injured and still in the hospital. He thought that was terrible and was so sorry to hear about that. He said he never knew much about them, but they had always seemed nice to him, and he hoped that Jody would soon be over all of that.

The balance of the drive back was what their thoughts were about each other. Greg said to her, "Erika, you must know that I like you very much and can't get you off my mind even when I'm working."

"Oh, I'm sorry, I don't want to interfere with your work, I do like you also. I think you are a very nice gentleman, and I enjoy being with you."

At that, he gave her a kiss on the cheek. She could feel the blood race to her face. This was another first for her. She had never experienced a man's lips on her before, and she liked it. She didn't think she would ever forget that outing with Greg. It was so wonderful and unusual for her.

As they arrived at the apartments, Erika said to him," I think I'll stop and see Dan before I go up and see how everything is going for him."

"I'll join you," he said

They knocked on Dan's door and he opened it. He looked very bad, like he hadn't slept for a week.

"How is Jody?" Erika asked.

"She is a little better today," he answered.

"You know Greg Watson, Dan? He lives down the hall," she said, introducing Greg to him.

"Oh yes, I've seen him go in and out. Hi Greg, they think Jody will be well enough to come home tomorrow, and I will have her friend stay with her for awhile." He said to them.

"Oh, good," Erika said. "I was wondering if she had someone to help if she came home."

"If there is anything we can do, just let us know," Greg offered.

Dan thanked him and said that was nice of him. Erika also thought that was a very nice gesture.

Greg accompanied Erika to her door and as he started to leave, she invited him in for a cup of coffee or tea. He accepted her invitation, and she offered him a seat while she prepared the coffee.

Darcy was not at home, so they felt that they had a little privacy.

Erika served the coffee, and just then the phone rang. Erika answered and it was Darcy on the other end.

"Hi Erika, I'm going to be home a little late and so you don't worry about me, I'm going to the movies with a friend I met today, OK?"

"Well, you be very careful and I will see you later," she warned her and hung up the phone.

Getting back to Greg and their coffee, she repeated what Darcy said to her on the phone. He looked at her with a smile on his face and said, "I hope I'm not being selfish, but I'm glad she is going to be late. Now we can be alone for awhile."

He was sitting on the sofa and she in a chair across from him. Soon he came over to her and took her hand and very gently led her over next to him on the sofa.

"Why are you doing this?" she asked.

"I want you close to me so that I can kiss you and put my arms around you and embrace you," he said as he pulled her closer to him and pressed his lips to hers.

Oh my goodness! She thought, I have never had a feeling like that before. She had never been kissed like that on the mouth.

Then he asked, "Erika, have you ever had anyone make love to you?"

"You mean like that? No, I have never had anyone kiss me like that before."

"I mean, did anyone ever go any further in love-making with you?"

She looked up at him and with that feeling again like she was drowning in his pale, blue eyes. She was beginning to melt but knew she shouldn't. She thought that she had better explain to him before he went too far with his intentions.

"Greg, I come from a very strict religious family and was very sheltered in that respect, and this is the first time the opposite sex has ever imposed on my feelings. And I must tell you that I like it extremely well, and I like you, but the feelings must not go any further because I am afraid it may go too far," she said, even though she still had a desire for him to continue.

He told her he appreciated her frankness, but still wanted to make love to her. She told him even though she was having the same feelings, she couldn't allow it to go any further. She said she still would like to continue to see him and get to know him better. He said he knew that if she would allow him the privilege, he would still have a desire to see her.

When he felt that he couldn't proceed with his feelings, he thought it best to bid her goodnight and asked if he could see her again.

"Yes, Greg, I would like that," she said, and though he was imposing on her, he kissed her on the lips and said goodnight and left.

Would he ever call on her again? She wondered.

She was to find out the next morning when he called her. He told her he really enjoyed the day with her yesterday and hoped that he didn't insult her by his advances last night.

She said, "No, Greg. I didn't feel that it was an insult but rather a compliment, but you must understand how I feel."

"Yes, I do Erika, and I must apologize for coming on that strong so soon before we really had a chance to know each other better."

"Thank you Greg and I accept your apology," she said.

"And you will let me see you again?" he asked.

"Of course," she answered, knowing deep in her heart that she had the desire to see him again.

This morning was Sunday and she just wanted to stay in bed and think of Greg, so after he called she cuddled up to stay a little while longer. It felt so good.

Soon she heard Darcy stirring around in the kitchen, and she got up and went out to see what she was up to.

Darcy said, "Guess what? With some of the things Rod left here there's a waffle iron, and I think I'll make waffles this morning for our breakfast. How does that sound to you?"

"Wow, that sounds good to me," Erika said. "By the way, who did you go to the movies with last night?" she asked.

"Oh she was one of the ladies I met at the employment agency. She lives close by here, and we got to talking, and I knew you would be out with Greg. So I agreed to her invitation."

"Incidentally, I think I'm going to accept that job with the jewelry store. I understand the items are very high price, so the commissions will be good." She said.

"Oh, yes, I think that is wise. Now let's have those scrumptious, waffles I'm starving," Erika said.

"By the way, how was your outing yesterday? Did you drown in Greg's eyes again?" Darcy asked with a big giggle.

"He is such a sweet man, and I really like him, but I need to shy off from him for a little while as he wants to come on a little strong with me. I must concentrate on my work if I want it to get ahead. Ian is counting on me."

"I know what you mean," Darcy agreed. "What are your plans for today?" she asked.

"I think I'm just going to check on some of my drawings that I have here. What are your plans, Darcy?"

"I thought I might go down and see how Dan is doing and how Jody is coming along. Wasn't he going to bring her home today?"

"Yes, I think that's what Dan said yesterday. We should check on that. That's a good idea." Erika said

While Darcy cleaned up the kitchen after their breakfast, Erika went to her drawing board and worked on some sketches for the gown she was designing.

The next morning was a work day for Erika, and Darcy was keeping her appointment with the jewelers. She said that she would call Erika at the studio after her consultation and let her know how it turned out.

The next day, as Erika was going over her drawings at the studio and looking at the beautiful outfits she was working on, her thoughts went again to her wardrobe and her date with Rod for dinner and theatre.

That was going to be in a couple of days and what was she going to wear? She asked herself. The only thing she had that was nice would be her new outfit she had made recently that was beige. She looked very chic in it, but would it be appropriate for the theatre? Well, it was the best that she had right now so it would have to be that outfit.

She decided to show Ian the drawing of her outfit and get his opinion. He looked at it and agreed that it was smart looking enough for the theatre and dinner.

Just then, the phone rang, and Ian picked it up. "It's for you Erika," he said as he handed the phone to her.

She took the phone, and it was Darcy. "I got the job," she heard her say with a very excited tone, "and they are very pleased with my hands, said I would be perfect to model the large diamond rings and necklaces."

"Oh I'm happy for you." Erika said. "Glad you called. I'll see you tonight, Bye."

After she hung up, she called to Ian to have him take a look at her sketch for the gown the lady requested for the installation benefit. He scanned over it and gave her a few critiques and then told her she was doing beautifully and the fabric she chose was perfect. "Keep up the good work," he said.

When she arrived at home, she thought she would check with Dan and see if he brought Jody home from the hospital today. She wasn't sure if Darcy had checked or not.

She knocked on his door and he opened and greeted her with, "Hi Erika."

"I just stopped by to see if Jody made it home and how she is doing," she said.

"No Erika, they would not release her yet. It seems she has an extreme psychological problem stemming from her trauma, and they would like that to be diminished before they release her."

"Oh, Dan, I'm so sorry, I thought she was doing real well but that doesn't sound good. Do they have any idea how long it will take?" she asked as she squeezed his hand, with a sympathetic gesture again.

"No, they say it will have to take its course."

"Have you had dinner yet?" she asked, and he said, "No, I just got home and haven't felt like fixing anything to eat."

"I'll tell you what. I'm going upstairs and preparing a dinner for Darcy and I, and I'll prepare a plate for you and bring it down. Would that be alright?"

"Thank you, Erika, that's real sweet of you but don't go to a lot of trouble."

"I won't, and I'll see you later," she assured him as she headed for her apartment.

While she was preparing the dinner for all of them, Darcy came in and asked, "Did you stop by and check with Dan, when you came in?"

"Yes, I did, and the hospital says Jody is not ready to be released yet. She has a mental problem due to the trauma," Erika informed her.

"That's terrible," Darcy said.

"I agree, and I told Dan that we would send down some dinner that I am making for us. I thought you might take it down if you don't mind. Would you?"

"Oh yes, then I can talk to Dan also," Darcy agreed

As soon as Erika had the dinner prepared, Darcy took the plate of food down to Dan.

Twenty minutes passed and Darcy hadn't returned; finally an hour passed and Erika had eaten her dinner and cleaned up the kitchen and still no Darcy.

Erika began to wonder, where was Darcy? Would she and Dan become cozy with each other? She hoped they weren't carrying this too far. After all, Dan needed someone now.

Finally, after an hour, Erika was planning to retire when Darcy came in the door with the empty plate.

"My goodness, I was beginning to worry about you," she said to Darcy

"Oh, the time seemed to go by so fast, and we were having such a good conversation, I never realized it was this late. I really enjoyed talking to him, and he insisted he share the dinner with me. He said he wasn't very hungry and that was a large plateful. He is such a nice man, and I feel sorry he is going through this problem. I told him I would check on him tomorrow."

"That was nice of you, Darcy. And how did you do on your first day at selling diamonds?" she asked.

"I didn't sell anything today; I was just a trainee, but they say I will do well. I sort of got the hang of it today pretty well, and I like it."

"I'm glad you're happy with it," Erika said.

Erika then told Darcy, now that they both had settled down with their new jobs she was going to put all her energy into her designing work. She loved the work that she was doing, and she said Ian was patient with her, and she appreciated that. He was very satisfied with the commissioned jobs he had given to her, and she felt that she must continue her good work.

He told her he was going to have that special fashion show soon, and he wanted her to have some of her designs ready to put into the show also. He was so pleased in how her designs were looking now. He thought she was almost ready to show them. He also said he was getting ready to make a trip to Asia for the special fabrics, so Erika made up her mind that she was going to work very hard.

She had almost all of her working tools at the studio now so that meant she would need to spend a lot more time at the studio, and she wouldn't have the time to see Greg very often.

Well, maybe it is better that way, I won't have to brush him off from coming on so strong, she thought to herself.

But she still had that big night out with Rod for dinner and the theatre. She had been sort of concerned about what she was going to wear but Ian convinced her that her other new outfit was fine. It was the dress she had made—beige, finely woven wool with three-quarter length sleeves and a flap type collar that folded out over the sleeveless vest-type jacket that she made in a small plaid in corresponding colors. So that was settled in her mind.

She wondered what it would be like to be out socially with Rod. She always just thought of him as her landlord. She would find out in a couple of days. Then she got back to her work on her designs.

After work she went shopping for the accessories to go with her outfit. She was shopping for new shoes, and they would need to be in a very conservative style because she had been used to the old Amish styles, and gradually she was breaking herself into the more stylish type but couldn't quite handle the very high heels as yet. So she was sticking to the medium heels for now.

She found something she thought would be perfect to go with her new outfit. They were of very soft suede in beige with heels just like she wanted. She decided they would be dressy enough for the evening. Now, she just had to wait for the day after tomorrow. The more she thought of it the more excited she became. To see a stage show was something she had never experienced before. She found that a lot of people were talking about the stage show "Oklahoma" and decided it must be special.

When she reached home, she expected to see Darcy there but she hadn't come in yet.

She wondered where she could be. Then the phone rang, and it was Darcy. "Hi, I thought you would be home. I'm down at Dan's. I stopped by to see how he was doing," she said.

"That's a good idea. I just got home and I wondered where you were. I should have known that you would be with him. Do you think it is getting pretty regular?" Erika said to her."

"I hope not," Darcy said

Erika proceeded to make herself some dinner and prepared enough for Darcy. After she had finished her dinner, Darcy still hadn't come in, so she cleaned up the kitchen and went into her bedroom and looked over her new outfit and the shoes she had just purchased. Then she prepared to go to bed.

She had just fallen asleep when she heard Darcy come in.

"Are you asleep?" Darcy asked

"Oh, almost, I was just about there when I heard you come in. How was your day?"

"It was great," Darcy told her. "I sold my first diamond ring today. It was just a "pinkie" ring, but it had several diamonds in it, and it was a pretty large ring for a pinkie because the lady who purchased it was a large lady with pretty large fingers."

"And how was Dan? Have they decided when Jody would come home?" Erika asked.

"No, they don't know how much longer she will need to stay there, and I told him I would see him tomorrow after work. I'll stop and bring a pizza for the two of us."

"It seems like you are enjoying your visits with Dan, are you getting to like him?" Erika asked.

"Yes, you might say that. He is a very sweet guy, and I enjoy being with him. I hope you aren't getting too worried about Dan and me. I do like him a lot, and I guess I just want to help him," Darcy said.

"Oh, oh, watch out. But then, you are a big girl, and you should know what you are doing, right?" Erika said to her

"Yes, I hope I do." Darcy replied

Erika knew Darcy, and she wasn't too concerned about her, but what about Dan? Was he missing the opposite sex right now? Would Darcy be able to reject his advances since she was getting to like him more as time went on? She hoped she could.

"When are you going out with Rod, is it tomorrow night or the next night?"

"It is the next night, on Wednesday." Erika told her. "That is when I will find out what kind of a person he is and just what his intentions are. I am very curious."

After they had gone to bed, Erika stretched out and laid there thinking about Rod. What kind of a man was he and would he treat her with respect, or would he come on strong the first time with her. She'd just have to wait and see.

The next night Darcy did stop and see Dan again, and she brought a pizza for them both and enjoyed spending the full evening with him. She was beginning to give him a part of her heart. He was becoming very affectionate with her, and she was being receptive to his advances. She liked him very much, and it was becoming hard for her to leave him, and he was on her mind a lot.

Erika spent the evening preparing all of her attire for the next evening with Rod. She wanted to look her very best for him. Why? He hadn't made any advances toward her. Was she trying to win him over? She asked herself. She did want to find out if there was someone special in his life and just what he thought of her and why he was so nice to her.

The following day she received a phone call from Rod, and he said, "If it is convenient for you to leave work a little early, I will pick you up at six p.m. Will that be alright? Will that give you enough time to get ready by six?"

"Yes, thank you, Rod and I will see you at six p.m."

She left the studio around three p.m. and had plenty of time to go home and be ready for Rod.

When she had showered and had her make-up on, she decided she would style her hair differently—She thought she would make some braids pulling them towards the back above her ears letting more of her pretty blonde hair fall beneath the braids, going to the back of her head toward the nape of her neck and put a large brooch at the end of the braids. She then brought the short hair in the front over her brow to the left as a shaggy bang. It looked really good to her, and it was something she hadn't done before. Then she continued to dress with her new beige dress that she had made recently and that Ian had confirmed would be suitable for the dinner and show.

She had just finished dressing when there was a knock on the door. She went to answer it, thinking for sure it was Rod. She opened the door, and there he stood so handsome in his dress clothes. He was wearing dark brown pants with very sharp creases and wearing a brown jacket with a pretty brown, with gold and copper patterns in the tie.

"My you look lovely this evening," he said as he ushered her to the stairs.

And she answered as her heart was fluttering madly. "Thank you sir, and you look very handsome this evening also." She decided then that his outfit was perfect to go with her outfit and together they made a very handsome couple.

As he led her to the car, she noticed that he was driving a different car, not the convertible she had seen before.

"What happened to the red convertible I saw you driving before?" she asked.

"Oh, I still have that. I decided to take this one tonight as I may need to have it valet parked, and I don't care to have them drive the convertible."

After they were seated comfortably in the car, he told her that they would have dinner at Auriole's restaurant as it was not far from the theater and their menu was very good.

Then Erika informed him. "It would make no difference to me because I have not eaten at a restaurant since I arrived, and I hope it is not too high-class as I haven't had much experience at that."

"Now don't you worry your pretty head about that, you are a beautiful lady and look so lovely that when they see you they won't think a thing about class. Besides, I will be there to support you if you need help. And I will see that you enjoy it, and I will enjoy every minute with my lovely lady."

Everything seemed to go alright during their dinner. They talked about each other's lives prior to now. He told Erika that he was from northern New York State and that he worked on Wall Street with stocks and bonds. He had been in that work for two years now and seemed to be doing well.

He also asked more about her fashion designing and how she liked the new job. She told him how she acquired the position and about her new boss and his feminine actions. When he heard that, he gave her a big smile and squeezed her hand.

After dinner, which she found very delicious and elegantly served amidst the ambience of this fabulous restaurant, Rod informed her that it was off to the theater and the show. Erika was all excited as this was the first theater and first stage show that she had ever seen.

The theater was packed with many people milling around. She wondered where they all came from. Soon the curtain started to rise and the music began. The show was starting. She had never heard such wonderful music before. She sat there wide-eyed all during the show. What a show it was. The music was wonderful with songs like, "Oh what a Beautiful Morn'in," which was a waltz; and also "People will say we're in love" and "Surrey with a fringe on top." All the songs they sang were songs that she liked. The setting was kind of a reminder of her upbringing on the farm. Erika had never seen anything like it in her whole life. It was magnificent to her. The singing and the dancing held her spellbound.

Rod was fascinated by her intrigue. It was something that she would never, ever forget.

During the intermission, Rod escorted her to the lobby and treated her to a drink. Then it was back to the show for the ending.

After the show, he led her to a very elegant lounge just off the lobby and asked her if she would like a drink or something. She answered him and said, "Whatever you want, but I will have an apple cider if they have it, thank you."

He looked at her as if to apologize for his offer, but ordered the cider for her and a martini for himself, and surprisingly, they did have the cider and served it to her. When they served it, he looked at her lovingly and reached over and kissed her on the cheek. His lips were very warm to her cheek and gave her a thrill.

After they had finished their drink, they went out to order the car. When the valet delivered it, he helped her in and went around and entered the driver's seat. Just like a gentleman would do, she thought. Would he always treat her like a lady, she wondered?

On the way to the apartment, he put his arm around her and pulled her over close to him. It seemed just like Greg had done. He had the radio playing soft, romantic music. The car was beautiful, and the music was beautiful, and the show was wonderful. What else could a person ask for? Then he spoke and broke the silence.

"Do you need to go directly home?" he asked.

"Well, tomorrow is a work day for me, why do you ask?" she answered.

"I thought you might like to see the apartment that I have now, since we go right past the building to take you home."

She was surprised by the offer and said to him, "Rod, do you have other ideas for this night? I really enjoyed the whole evening, and I enjoyed being with you, but I don't want anything to spoil it."

"Erika, I wouldn't do anything to hurt you or that you wouldn't want me to do and if you don't want us to stop by, just say no and I won't. Your wishes are my command, my sweet lady."

Erika thought awhile. Since he had given her such a great evening, what harm could it be if they just stopped by for a few minutes? So she agreed and told him, "Just for a few minutes, Rod."

His apartment was in a very high-class neighborhood, and it had an elevator to go up to his apartment. It wasn't a penthouse, but it was way up there, and when they entered the apartment, she could see all of the other tall buildings lit up and all the city lights. It was really dazzling and kind of made her feel a little dizzy to look out of the window to the street below. What beautiful furnishings he had, but that didn't surprise her, knowing the furnishings he had in the apartment that she rented from him. He offered her a seat on a very plushy sofa. Then he placed a very pretty crystal dish of fine chocolates on the coffee table in front of her and offered her one.

She proceeded to compliment him on the décor of his apartment and kept looking around and asked him if he had any help in the decorating.

He said that he had been going with a lady who was an interior decorator, and she helped him, combining a few of his touches here and there.

Erika asked if he was still seeing the lady and he said, "No, we have ended our relationship some time ago."

As they were talking, he came over and sat next to her on the sofa. After a little while, he put his arm around her and squeezed her to him. She liked his touch very much and he gave her another squeeze. This time he found her lips and brought his lips down on hers. They were red hot and she couldn't resist and gave her lips to him freely. What am I doing? This feeling is so wonderful that I don't want him to quit. Does he really have loving feeling for me? Or is this a pastime? This is not how I expected this to be, but I like it very much. Could I be falling in love with him? I had better have him take me home before it goes too far.

Then she said to him. "Rod, I think you had better take me home, what do you think?"

"Yes, I think you are right, I just couldn't resist kissing you I have wanted to do that and hold you in my arms ever since I met you and it was worth the wait. But I will honor your wishes this time."

When they got to her apartment, she thanked him for the outstanding time he had shown her and gave him a kiss on the cheek. Then he cupped her face in his hands and found her lips for a passionate kiss on her lips. He wasn't settling for a kiss on the cheek. His feelings for her went deeper than that. He told her he wanted to see her again soon if she would allow that. Then she told him that she was going to knuckle down with her work for awhile because she believed that she needed to do that with the fashion show coming up and her work was too important to her.

He asked her if he could call her in the evening when she wasn't working. She said, "Yes, of course." With that he bid her goodnight and headed for the stairs to depart.

When she came into the apartment, Darcy wasn't there, but there was a note from her saying that she was down at Dan's.

Oh well, she thought, Darcy might just as well enjoy herself too. Although she hoped she wasn't getting too involved with Dan. It would be easy for her to do since she was beginning to like him very much, and Dan needed someone.

She was tired and tomorrow was another work day, so she went to bed

She lay there thinking about the wonderful evening she had just spent with Rod and how wonderfully he treated her. Did he treat every woman that well? And was he still seeing that interior decorator he mentioned? For a split second, she felt a little pang of jealousy strike her. Wow, what is wrong with me? Why did it bother me? He is not committed to me, she thought.

She didn't hear Darcy come in she must have been fallen sound asleep.

The next morning she didn't hear Darcy moving around so she

peeked into her room to see if she was awake. Whoops! There was no Darcy, and the bed hadn't been slept in. It looks like she is enjoying Dan's company more and more, or is it Dan enjoying Darcy's company and needing some of her affections? Well she will probably hear one way or the other when she sees Darcy.

When she got to the studio, she was a little early, and Ian hadn't come in yet, so she went right to work on her drawings. When Ian came in, he asked her how her date was with Rod. He knew she was going out with him and that he was taking her to see the Oklahoma stage show.

She said, "Oh, Ian, it was fabulous. I have never experienced anything like it before in my life. He also took me to the most elegant restaurant—Auriole's—have you heard of it?"

"Have I heard of it? Yes, and it is one of the best. It looks like he likes the best of everything. He should when he is courting one of the most beautiful and best ladies ever." Erika blushed and looked embarrassed and thanked him for the compliment.

Over the next few weeks, she was very busy making many gowns. They were to be for the orders they were commissioned to do for the seasonal parties at Christmas that the very important people were having, and time was drawing near. Also, she was preparing for Ian's fashion show that was coming up soon.

She hadn't seen Greg or Rod for quite some time because she was so busy with her work. She did receive a couple of calls from Greg, and he asked if he could see her, and she declined because of her work. He said he understood and asked if she would mind if he called her occasionally to check and see if she could find time. She told him, no, she wouldn't mind. She was so busy that sometimes she was very late getting home and didn't see much of Darcy.

One night, when she got home, Darcy was there for a change, and it surprised her. "Well, this is a surprise, I haven't seen you for some time, what have you been up to?" she asked. She knew very well what Darcy had been up to. It was Dan.

"Just work with nothing very exciting," her friend answered

"Have you seen Dan lately? Erika asked.

"Yes, I saw him a few nights ago, and he said Jody was coming home tomorrow and thought we had better cool it with us being together so often."

"What did he mean by that?" Erika asked

"He just said not to come down so often when Jody comes home; she might get the wrong idea about the two of us and to wait until she was better."

"What kind of a wrong idea could she get from you visiting them?" Erika asked.

"Well, Dan and I have been very close, and I mean very close, lately. We are both becoming very attached to each other, and it might show, and she may become very suspicious, especially with her mental problem. He must handle her with kid gloves, so to speak."

Then Erika said. "Darcy, maybe it would be a good idea for you to find someone else to take up your free time for awhile." Darcy agreed to that.

Erika decided to change the subject. She wasn't sure she would like to hear any more of what was going on with Darcy and Dan. She asked, "How is your new job going, Darcy?"

"It's great. I am selling more top quality jewelry now and making more commissions, which makes me very happy. I really like the job."

As they talked more about her job, she told Erika about a salesman who was coming into the store and asked her out several times. She didn't know whether to accept or not. She didn't know much about him, although he seemed like a very nice guy.

Erika asked her, "Does anyone in the shop who you could talk to know anything about him? Maybe you could find out a little information about him?"

"I don't know. I have never asked anyone because I didn't want them to know that he asked me out," she answered.

Erika then said to her, "Maybe you should accept his invitation, and it may make you forget about Dan. I know you are hurt because he asked you to cool it."

Darcy gave her a sad grin and shook her head in agreement then said, "Goodnight, I'm going to bed. See you in the morning."

A few weeks passed, and Erika caught up with making the party dresses and was beginning to work on designs for the fashion show. She was doing very well, and Ian praised her work every day. He also picked out some of her designs that he thought he would like in the show, and she was to select the fabric she thought was appropriate for the gowns. When she selected the fabrics, she draped them on a manikin to show how she thought they could be used. Then she showed them to Ian, and he approved of the work she was doing with the fabrics, and told her she was doing a great job. Now all she had to do was direct the fabricators, Roger and Betsy, and have the gowns made just like she wanted them to be.

A few days later she was working with her design on a manikin when she got a phone call, and it was Rod Burton. "Erika, I must see you. Do you think you can see me tonight after work?"

"What is it, Rod? Is something wrong? Is this important?"

"It is very important to me, but I don't know how important it is to you, but I really want to see you tonight," he answered

"Rod, you know that I am getting ready for the big fashion show, and I am very busy right now."

"I'm sorry to interfere with your work darling, but couldn't you just see me for a few minutes?

After you have finished your work? I'll come by and pick you up at the studio. I promise I won't keep you long."

"Well, alright if you promise not to keep me too late," she agreed. What in the world could he want that would be so important? She thought.

He was there to pick her up in the red convertible, and it was a good thing that she brought her scarf along. She knew her hair would blow all over if he had the convertible.

"Rod, you acted as though this is a real urgency," She said to him. Without saying a word he drove a little way and came to a stop along the curb.

A Runway For A Dream

He put his arms around her and said, "Erika, I don't know what your feelings are for me but my feelings are driving me crazy. I can't get you off my mind, and I think I have fallen in love with you. The night that we went to the show and dinner, when we were at my place, I wanted to take you so badly. But I felt it would be against your wishes, so as hard as it was to refrain, I knew I had to. Erika, I just need to know what your feelings are for me. I realize that you are real busy now, but do you think you care enough for me to make me a priority in your social life when your social life doesn't interfere with your work?" He gave a kittle laugh.

Oh, what a position he has put me in at this time, she thought. After a few moments of mulling it over in her mind, she answered him: "Rod, I like you very much and truly enjoy your company and hope to keep seeing you, but you need to understand this—I have only been away from my roots less than one year and the whole idea of me coming here was to broaden my knowledge in fashion designing, and I think you know that, and that is my goal. If, in the meantime, I can afford a nice social life, there are some people that I would like to include in my life and you are one of them, but I can't say that you are the only one. In other words what I am saying is, socially I will need space and time to become adjusted to my new life here, and during that time, you will be one of those at the top of my list of priorities." He listened to her intently and was looking at her with an endearing smile all the time she was talking to him. "Does that help you with your question, and does that give you an idea as to how I feel about you?"

When she was all through telling him how she felt, he put his arm around her and squeezed her to him and said, "Erika, you are one in a million, and I can't help but agree with you on all you've said, but I still can't help feeling the way I do about you, and if you don't mind, I will still hang in there."

"Thank you, Rod, and I will respect the way you feel also."

She reached over, and with her hand on his cheek, she kissed him on the lips. That felt very good to her and surprised her to have found the courage to make that bold a gesture, but decided she liked it.

With that, she said she needed to get home and wanted to go back to the studio and get some of her things. He said he would take her home after that.

When they went back to the studio, they noticed two men sitting in the lobby, and one of them was her boss, Ian. Erika had never seen the other man before. The other man had his arm around Ian and their faces were pretty close to each other. Rod asked Erika if she knew who the other man was, and she said, "No, I have never seen him around here before"

Rod looked at her sort of funny and said, "They look and act like they are lovers."

When the men saw them, they immediately separated, and Ian looked embarrassed and said to Erika, "Is something wrong? I thought you had left for the day."

"Oh, I'm sorry, I had an errand and just came back to pick up some things."

When they left the lobby and went into the studio, Rod repeated what he said to her in the lobby. Then Erika said to him very quietly, "I have had suspicions that Ian was different because he was only attracted to men, never women, but I never saw him do anything out of line."

"Well, it does not concern us, so we'll just leave them alone. What do you say?"

"I say you're right, Rod."

When they passed through the lobby to leave, Ian and his friend were not there

Rod continued to take Erika home, and as he took her to her door, he said," I hope you don't make me wait too long to see you again." Then he gave her a very passionate kiss on the lips, which she readily returned, and said, "I'll try not to. Goodnight dear Rod, thank you for bringing me home."

When she got inside, she saw that Darcy was at home, so she said, "Hi, how was your day, did you check with Dan and Jody to see how they are doing?"

Darcy answered, "Yes I stopped by, and Dan answered the door and came out in the hall to talk to me. He said Jody is healing up physically, but she is still bad, mentally. She doesn't want Dan to come near her sexually. She has become kind of withdrawn and sort of suspicious of him, thinking he is seeing someone else. She says she feels too tainted to come near him. He just lets her go her own way. She sits around and keeps in deep thought. He says he doesn't know how to handle her. I asked him if she suspected me, and he said he didn't think she did, but he couldn't tell what she was thinking. He is thinking of going to a psychiatrist and seeing what advice he gets from him."

"Maybe that is a good idea," Erika said to Darcy. "That's what I told him," Darcy said

When Erika went to bed, after talking to Darcy, she laid there thinking about her plans.

She decided that she was going to spend a lot more time with her work.

The next few weeks she did just that. She was doing fine and had several designs made up ready to be fabricated. Now she had to choose the experienced models she wanted, who would walk down the runway and model her designs in the fashion show. Her designs had to fit the models perfectly.

The show was just a few weeks away. She felt that she was ready, and Ian agreed with her. Everything seemed to be coming along fine for her, and outside of her work, she had seen Rod and Greg a few times very casually and conversed with them on the phone often, but she kept her work as a priority.

One evening, when she arrived at the apartment and checked her mail, she saw a letter and noticed it was from Rachel, her sister back home. As soon as she got in the door she opened it in a hurry; she was anxious to see what she had to say. As she read it, she was taken back with the news that was in there. Her sister said their mother was very ill and could she come home; she wanted to see her.

Erika never dreamed that she would get an urgent call to go back home. What worried her right now was the fact that in order for her to get there in a hurry, she would need to fly there, and she had never been in an airplane before in her life. As she thought about it, she knew it was a necessity.

She wanted to talk to someone who might have some experience in flying, and the only one that came to her mind was Rod. She called him, and he told her not to be afraid, that she would probably find it necessary to fly in the future also if she intended to continue with her business. He told her to take care, that she would be OK, and he would take her to the airport to depart and be there waiting for her when she returned.

She understood that he was right in what he said about flying, but she was still a little nervous and thought she would let Greg know that she was going to be gone for a few days. Greg said that he would miss her and hoped that all would be OK with her parents. She had already told Ian that she would be gone, hopefully for just a few days.

Then in planning what to wear, she decided she would wear a very conservative outfit and also take very conservative clothing so she wouldn't seem out of place with her people.

Rod took her to the airport and tried to calm her nerves about flying, and he kissed her and embraced her until she boarded the plane, hoping that would make her feel better.

When she arrived in Lancaster, she took a cab out to the farm. The other farmers noticed the cab bringing her, and all the neighbors looked at her with wonderment.

Her sister greeted her and informed her of her mother's problem and said it didn't look very good.

After seeing her mother she knew then why they asked her to come home. She had no idea that her mother had been ill. They had never contacted her telling of her illness.

It seemed that as soon as her mother saw her, she seemed satisfied that her wish had been fulfilled. She held Erika's hand and said to her with a very soft voice. "My child, I hope your coming here this time does not jeopardize your work, as I don't want to interfere. I know you have worked very hard to get where you are, and my prayers were for you. I always wanted your dream to come true."

"Mama, you are important to me, and I love you for standing by me all of those years with my dream, and now I want you to get well," Erika said as she kissed her mother on the cheek.

Her mama smiled and patted her hand and said, "I'll be back in shape in no time, you will see."

Erika could see that it wouldn't be long, and she was right, it wasn't. The very next day her mother passed on, and after Erika helped the rest of the family with all the arrangements, she made preparations to return to New York and her work. It was a sad departure for her to leave her father and siblings. She had been gone five days from her work now and felt that she needed to get back to it. There was so much ahead for her to do.

Greg knew when her flight was coming in so he was there to greet her when she arrived. What a prince he is, she thought!

Then he insisted they stop and have dinner before he took her home. He chose a very cute little café where they could sit and have an intimate conversation. He felt that he wanted to be alone with her for a little while before taking her home.

After a lot of persuasion from him, she had a glass of wine, her first with him, and it gave her a very warm feeling going down to add to the other feeling she was getting when she looked into his eyes. When the dinner and talk were completed, he said he better take her home because he knew she was tired and needed the rest. She was beginning to feel the results of the two glasses of wine and agreed with him.

When they arrived at their apartments, he asked if she would like to come into his apartment while he changed into something more casual before going upstairs. He had gone to the airport directly from his office and was still wearing his business suit. She agreed. She just realized how tired she was. It had been a very stressful five days for her.

He said for her to have a seat and excuse him while he went into the bedroom to change.

Erika found the sofa and flopped down on it. She was trying hard to keep her eyes open, waiting for him, and she thought she would just close them for a minute, hoping she wouldn't let herself go to sleep

It wasn't more than a few minutes when she felt his presence next to her and opened her eyes, and there he was, looking directly into her eyes. Looking into his eyes, she had a sense of drowning again. She seemed to have no resistance of him. He put his lips to hers with a very passionate kiss. This time, she couldn't resist him. He pressed her body so close to him that she could hardly breathe, but she was ecstatic and loved every minute of it with the desire for more. For the next few minutes, she was oblivious to everything but that wonderful sensation of drowning in his love. This was the first time she had ever experienced any feelings like this, and she didn't quite know what to think or where to go from there. He was so gentle and caring, and while she had tears in her eyes, he looked at her and said, "Don't cry sweet Erika, I'm so sorry and didn't mean to make you cry, but I just couldn't hold back any longer. I have wanted to love you ever since I met you."

"No Greg, you didn't hurt me, but it was so beautiful. It gave me a feeling that I have never in my life experienced before—and will always remember."

He drew her body up close to his and kissed her passionately on the lips again and held them there.

Then coming back to realization, she said, "Greg, I think I had better go to my apartment now, and there will be no need for you to come upstairs. I can make it OK."

"Are you alright?" he asked.

"Yes, I am fine," she answered.

"May I call you later?" he asked.

"Yes, if I haven't fallen asleep." He opened the door for her exit.

Oh boy, she didn't go to sleep for a very long time, thinking of the wonderful experience that she just had with Greg. She finally came to the conclusion that it must have been the past several days of stress with her family that caused her to lose resistance to all of these passionate advances. But what was that going to do to her plans?

She thought of Rod and what her feelings were for him. He wanted an answer from her about her feelings, could she give him any kind of an answer. If Greg approached her with the same question, could she give him an answer? Those were questions going on in her mind. Finally, she fell asleep.

She was anxious to see what went on at the studio the next day, so she was there bright and early. Ian wasn't there, and Roger said everything was just about ready for the show. The models she requested would be in tomorrow for Erika to approve.

She had just another week before the show, so she knew that her days would be full.

That meant she would not have any time for her socializing. So she had to buckle down and give her career all of her attention.

Rod called her and asked how her trip was and gave his condolences and asked when she thought he could see her. He said he had really missed her.

She thanked him for his concern and then informed him that she was going to be really busy until after the show. He seemed disappointed but said he understood and was looking forward to seeing her after the show was over. She laughed, and he said he meant every word he said.

Erika put all of her attention on the fashion show, but she did take a little time to check on Jody to see how she was doing. She only talked to Dan because Jody was sort of withdrawn and didn't like to come to the door. Dan said that she was still acting the same, and that he had talked to the psychiatrist, and he told him it would take more time. Dan said he didn't know how long he could handle it.

When she saw Darcy, she told her what Dan had said, and Darcy said, "Yes, Dan talked to me about that, and he wants to see me outside of their apartment somewhere. He said he needs me and has very deep feelings for me, and he is not getting any love or affection from his Jody and it's driving him crazy."

"Erika, I don't know what to do. I have very strong feeling for him and have refrained myself from getting too involved, but don't know how long I can keep away from him. I find that I am beginning to fall in love with him and want to be near him." Darcy said.

Erika studied her for a moment and then said to her, "Darcy, I know exactly how you feel, but you are in a very peculiar situation, and you must be careful. Jody is not herself, and you don't know what she might do."

"That is what worries me, and I told Dan I just had to stay away from him for awhile."

"I know as much as you hate to do that, it is the best way to handle it," Erika told her.

"I guess I will have to find someone who will take up my time and attention away from him," Darcy said to her

Then Erika thought to herself, someone should really talk to Jody and try to make her understand what she is doing to Dan. Maybe she would find the opportunity to talk to her; she was going to try and would also encourage Darcy to stay away from Dan. She felt that she didn't want to interfere, but Darcy and Dan needed to stay away from each other.

Then Darcy told her, "There is this one salesman who comes into the store, and he keeps asking to take me out, but I keep refusing because of the way I feel about Dan. Maybe if I let him take me out on a date he will keep my mind off Dan, and it will help," Darcy said.

"You're right. Let him take you out and show you the town and wine and dine you—that will keep your mind on something and someone besides Dan."

"I think that is what I will do. The next time he asks to take me out, I will accept his invitation," said Darcy.

Then Erika thought to herself—that seems to clear things up for Darcy but not for me. She was still all confused about Greg and Rod.

Chapter 3
A SUCCESSFUL SHOW

I t was one day before the designers' show, and Erika was getting more nervous. She discussed with Ian the name she was going to use as her trade name for her designs. Ian thought she should have something with a little more class and more appropriate for her beautiful creations. Then they came up with just changing the type of print of her name. "*Creations by Erika*" seemed to appeal to her much more. So that is what she chose to use. She had four creations to enter and Ian had three, and there were twelve total. One other designer had two and the other three had one each. Everyone was eager to see the new designs that they all had to show. Ian's models wearing his designs came down the runway and were shown first, and then the other designers and Erika's were shown last

On the show day, everything seemed to go perfectly. It was quite an elaborate affair with champagne cocktails and canapés being served, and Erika had designed a magnificent gown for herself in a vibrant sapphire blue velvet with one shoulder exposed and a wide strap of silver Lame' over the other shoulder and a very narrow empire bodice done in silver Lame' with a split on one side of the skirt from mid- thigh to the hem line, which was edged in silver threads Her outfit was complemented with her sapphire-blue slippers. Everyone raved about her gown and how beautiful she looked.

She had a sign made up to be seen as the models came down the runway to model her designs and it read **Creations by "Erika."** She was happy with that.

When she checked around to see who had attended, she spied Rod Burton sitting back in the corner, and it appeared that he was with a woman. The woman seemed very interested in what the models were showing. Erika's heart did a little flip at first when she noticed him and thought perhaps the lady that was with him was the Interior Decorator friend of his, but then she decided she was happy that he was with someone.

She wondered if Greg would show up, then she returned to give her attention to the show.

Darcy was there and came up to her, gave her a big kiss and congratulated her on her great designs. She told her that she thought the show was magnificent, and her designs stood out over all the rest. Erika thanked her and said, "Darcy you are just partial to my designs." Darcy laughed and said, "No Erika it's true."

The show was a great success, and she received many orders for her creations. Ian was overwhelmed with the many ovations she received as her models came down the runway showing her designs. He complimented her again and said it was because of the way she applied those special detailed touches that she gave each design. He said they were outstanding.

After the show she changed out of her gown into something more casual. As she was walking out, Rod greeted her and put his arm around her and gave her his congratulations. She noticed that he wasn't with the woman who was there during the show.

He asked if he could treat her to a "cider" and take her home.

She laughed at his remark, remembering the first time he offered to treat her to a drink, so she said to him, "Yes, you may treat me a white wine as I feel that it may relax me after all this. And I will accept your offer to take me home." She was pretty tired and glad to accept his offer.

He ushered her into the cocktail lounge that was close by and they found a table which was kind of secluded. He ordered her a glass of chardonnay and a martini for himself. While they were waiting to be served, she looked up toward the entrance and saw Greg go by, and he peered in and saw her and walked on.

She felt that he probably was hurt seeing her with another man, but hoped he wasn't too upset. After all, she had never made any commitments to him. Why hadn't she seen him at the show? She asked herself.

After a little talk about the show, Rod seemed to become more amorous and started to caress her on the back and arms, and she felt that he was preparing to ask her the questions he had asked her before about being her priority, and she knew she wasn't ready to answer him. So she thought it best to let him know now. She said to him, "Rod, have some consideration for me; please don't pressure me about that tonight. I will need more time. Do you understand what I am saying?"

"Yes, I do understand, but I want you to know that I was not just blowing wind. I meant every word of it. You are in my heart, and I can't get you out of my mind no matter how hard I try."

They had their drinks and made preparations to leave. Rod didn't have very much to say all the way to her apartment. He did ask her if she was going to work the next day and she said, "Yes,"

He also asked if she would see him again, and she said, "Of course." Since the show had started at three p.m. and was over at six p.m., it was still pretty early when she reached her apartment. Rod bid her goodnight with a kiss and left.

When she got inside, Darcy was there, and they talked over the show and about all the different designs that were shown. Darcy said to her, "I always told you that you were gifted with your art and knew you would go somewhere with it and that it could only be up." Erika thanked her for having that much confidence in her.

Soon the phone rang, and Darcy answered it. She handed the phone to Erika and said, "It's for you, and I think it is Greg."

Erika took the phone and said, "Hello? Oh, hi Greg. Thank you very much. Yes, I looked for you there but didn't see you. I was hoping you would see some of my creations. Oh you were. Where were you sitting? Thank you, it's nice of you to tell me that. I really can't say right now as I haven't figured what my schedule will be next week, but give me a call in a couple of days and I should know then. Thank you for saying that also. Goodnight Greg."

When she had finished her conversation and hung up the phone, Darcy was still sitting there with a quizzical look on her face, so Erika repeated the conversation to her.

"How long are you going to have him waiting for you?" Darcy asked.

"I haven't the slightest idea. I thought if I got myself all wrapped up in my work neither one of them would be able to handle it and they would both step back a little. I was hoping that they both would find someone to take up some of their time for a short while. I am torn between the two of them, and I know sexually Greg sends me to the moon. I just need to look into his eyes, and he's got me."

Rod, I adore, and he does something to me when he kisses me, and he is such a sweet gentleman, and I adore his mode of living.

At that, Darcy said, "Honey, I think you have your problems, as I do. I think I'm going to bed and forget about all of them." She waved her hands upward and headed toward her room.

Erika popped up and said to her, "Do you think if I went away for awhile and had some time to think about it, I would be able to make a decision?"

"That may be a good idea," Darcy agreed

Erika had a difficult time going to sleep that night. After all the excitement of the show and the thoughts of Rod and Greg, it was hard to clear her mind and relax. She finally dozed off and had wonderful dreams of her designs and all the people that were there to admire her new designs.

The next day at the studio, she and Ian discussed every phase of the show and planned on what they would do differently when they had the next one, which they both hoped for and looked forward to. She worked on her new designs all the rest of the day. Ian couldn't get over how well the show went.

She decided to go home early that night as she was pretty tired. It was kind of a let-down after the show so she went to bed early. Darcy wasn't home, and Erika surmised that she was probably with her new friend Brad after her work.

She must have fallen asleep because the next thing she knew, Darcy was shaking her and telling her to wake up, that she had something to tell her.

Erika sat up in bed and said, "What is it Darcy, what's wrong?"

"Well, I was just listening to the news on the radio and I heard them talking about Ian's design studio and that there was a murder there tonight. They didn't say who it was or give any details."

Erika jumped out of bed and immediately tried to call Ian, but it was not Ian. It was another man. "Hello, who is this?" the voice said.

"Who is this answering the phone?" she asked.

"Tell me who is calling?" he asked.

"This is Erika, and I work with Ian; is he there?'

"This is officer Grady with the police department. Would you please leave your name and phone number, and we will return your call?" So Erika gave him her number and hung up.

After she hung up, she said to Darcy, "I wonder what this is all about and who was murdered? And why are the police answering the phone?"

She couldn't think of anyone who would be in the studio who would be killed unless it was a burglar. Would they want to steal her designs and someone caught them in the act? What else could it be, she asked herself.

Darcy said, "We'll just keep listening to the news and see what we can find out.

"But I need to go into the studio in the morning and do some work," she told Darcy.

In just a few minutes the phone rang, and Erika answered it.

"Is this Erika Beiler?" the male voice asked.

"Yes, this is Erika."

"We would like to ask you some questions concerning a problem at the studio where you work. Could you come in to the studio? We will send a car to pick you up."

"Yes I will," she answered. "But can you tell me what this is all about?" she asked.

"We will clue you in to all the details when you come in," he said

She told Darcy what they wanted, and Darcy said, "I wonder who was murdered."

While Erika was preparing to leave, she was actually shaking in her shoes, she was so scared. Just before the policeman came to take her to the car, the phone rang again, and when she answered, it was Rod.

"Erika, darling, are you alright? I just heard the news, and I am worried about you. I think you need me to be there with you."

"Rod, I still don't know what this is all about, so I don't know what I need. The police just now phoned me and said they were sending a car to take me back to the studio. They would like to ask me some more questions. Oh, their car is here now, so I better go."

"I'll meet you there," he said

When she arrived at the studio, it was full of policemen, and cameramen were all over the place. She didn't see anyone she knew. Betsy the seamstress and Roger the cutter were not there. Finally, she couldn't stand it anymore and had to ask, "What is this all about and who was the person that was murdered?" Everyone looked at her almost with pity.

Then the officer, who was introduced to her as Sergeant Brady, came over to her and held her arm at the elbow and led her into the closed office. "Ma'am I am sorry to tell you this, but the man that was killed was your boss, Ian. He was shot to death."

He could see that she was about to faint, so he grabbed her around the waist and sat her down in a chair. At that moment, she looked out the door and saw Rod entering the studio. That seemed to calm her a bit. When Rod reached her, he asked the officer if she needed an attorney, and he said no; she was free to go. They had already checked her out and at this time, she was not a suspect, but he would like to ask her more questions that may shed some light on the case.

Rod came and sat next to her and held her hand while the officer asked all types of questions such as any business associates that Erika knew Ian had or people she thought he owed money to, or anyone she knew he had disagreements with, like his employees or clients—anything she could think of.

She said she couldn't think of anyone at that moment, but if she did, she would certainly inform him of it. Suddenly, she remembered the few disagreements that she heard him have with Roger and told the officer. "Ian was a sweet man and very dear to me and a hard worker in his business, so I don't know who would want to hurt him," she told the officer.

"Yes, we know about the arguments he had with Roger frequently and that Roger was jealous of the other lovers Ian had, but we checked out Roger, and he and Betsy are cleared as for as we can see. There are a couple more men out there who had designs on Ian's feelings, but we can't put our fingers on them as yet. If you can think of anyone would you please give us that information?"

"Yes, I certainly will. I can't believe anyone would want to do this to Ian," she repeated as they walked out of the studio.

"Who in the world would want to kill Ian?" she asked Rod, wiping away her tears.

"Well the kind of life he led with other men is an alarm for trouble," he said.

"Now, what do I do, Rod?" she asked.

"Oh my darling, I am so sorry you need to go through this, just when things were working out for you. Why don't you let me take you away for awhile until all of this clears up?"

"Oh Rod, you are so sweet and thoughtful, but I must figure out what I can do with my designing business. I can't just let it die out now."

"You're right, but I want to help you any way that I can. Will you allow me to do that?"

"Now I really need some time to think. Could we go someplace and have a drink? I feel that I need it to calm down my nerves," she pleaded. He directed her to a little bar close by and ordered a drink for both of them.

As they were sitting having their drinks, Erika looked over at Rod and said, "Why did this have to happen at this time, just when the big holidays are coming up. We had so many orders from the fashion show and for the Christmas and New Year's gowns. I have some, and I know Ian had a few, and they were all large commissioned deals. Now I don't have Ian to discuss all of this with. He was such a great help to me. I feel lost without him."

Rod put his arm around her and kissed her on the brow and he said, "Don't you fret about that just now, you will get it all figured out soon. You are a very strong and a very beautiful lady, and I have a lot of faith in you, and if you let me, I will stand by you and help you through all of this."

After he felt that she had calmed down a little, he decided he had better take her home. He took her to her apartment, and before he would let her go in, he embraced her and pressed his lips to hers then said, "Goodnight, darling," and left.

This had been a very stressful day for Erika, and when Darcy came home, she told her all about what had happened. She said to Darcy, "I don't know which way to turn now, if they let me back in the studio, do I still want to operate without Ian, and will Betsy and Roger still be allowed to work for me, and who will critique my work? Oh Darcy, I'm really going to miss Ian." At that, all of the pressure that had built up inside of her from the past incidents came out, and she began to cry. Darcy tried to console her and felt so sorry for her. Oh, how Erika wished that Rod was still there with her. She felt that she really needed him now.

Darcy came over to her and put her arms around her and said, "Erika, you don't need Ian or anyone to help you, and there are many people that you can discuss things with and who will give you a lot of support. You can just go on as you were and take care of all those orders, and everyone will love you for that, and you know you will make them very happy when they see your creations." After Darcy consoled her, she began to feel a lot better about where she was going with her plans.

When she finally got to bed, she was lying there thinking of what her next move would be. She decided she would ask the officials when she would be allowed to get back into the studio and if she could hire Betsy and Roger as her employees. If they would allow that, then maybe she could still continue to operate.

She did call them in the morning, and the sergeant advised her that she would need to wait another day or so until they got things more straightened out. He didn't have any problem with Betsy, but they weren't too sure about Roger yet because they were informed that there had been something between Roger and Ian prior to this time.

Erika decided to give Rod a call and see what he thought about her tentative plans.

She started to explain to him, and he stopped her in the middle and said, "Hold on

Sweetie, may I come over there? I think it will be a little easier for us to discuss this."

"OK, I'll make some coffee for us," she said.

In about forty-five minutes, he was there at her door. "How are you feeling, my darling?" he asked.

"You look like you have been crying."

"Oh Rod, I am so confused I don't know what to do."

"Sweetie, don't you worry your pretty head about what you are going to do. You know your work, and you know that people are crazy about your creations, and you can still continue to put them out, and I will be there beside you, whatever you do."

Then he enveloped her in his arms and pressed her close to him. She felt so protected with his arms around her. She told him about wanting to get the studio back so she could continue her work, and that the sergeant said they needed a few more days to keep working on finding the person who may have done this.

Then Rod sat up straight and with a definite tone said to Erika, "Do you remember the night that we saw Ian and that man in the lobby, and we thought it was sort of strange. Did you tell the officers about that?"

She gave him a surprised look and answered him, "Oh no Rod, I never thought about that anymore. I should call them and tell them what we saw."

"Yes you do that, and if they want me to confirm it, I will be glad to," he said.

"Fine, I'll call them right now and tell them I thought of something and will come in and see them when they want me to."

She immediately dialed the number and asked for the sergeant. As soon as he came on the line, she reiterated what she and Rod had talked about, and Rod popped up and said, "Also inform him that you have a witness to the fact." Then she repeated what Rod had just said.

After she had finished telling him that she had some information for him the sergeant asked her if she could come in to the station in the morning, and she agreed to be there.

After she hung up, she turned to Rod and said, "I'm sorry to have taken you away from your work again."

"That's not a problem. I wanted to be with you during this trying time for you. You know I don't like to see you hurt. Besides, I feel needed that way. Erika, I want you to need me." With that he pressed her closer to his body and with his free hand he cupped her soft chin and his warm lips met hers in a very long, passionate kiss. It was such a wonderful feeling she received from that kiss that she felt she didn't want it to end.

He released his embrace on her and said, "I'm so sorry—no I'm not—I loved every second of it and would do it again if you permitted."

"What makes you think you would not be permitted?" she asked.

"Well, Erika, you have been holding me off for so long, I was beginning to have the impression that you didn't like me at all."

"Oh Rod, that is not true. I do like you a lot, and you mean so much to me."

"Then, what is it Erika, why are you holding me off so long? You know that I love you dearly."

"I wish I could answer that for you Rod, but I just can't. I guess it's just that I want our relationship to be the perfect thing. I don't have any other answer right now."

"Well, that might hold me over for tonight, and you had better get some sleep. I'll call you in the morning and pick you up and go with you to the station."

He embraced her again and pressed his lips to hers. When he released her, he said, "I'll try to make that hold me until you make up your mind, and I hope it isn't too long."

She smiled at that, then she bid him goodnight, and he left.

Just as she was preparing to get into bed, Darcy came in, and she seemed all excited, and her face was all flushed. So Erika asked her. "What are you so excited about, Darcy?"

Darcy looked at her with a big smile and said, "Gee Erika, you won't believe this. That guy, the salesman, who comes into the store, today he came in and asked me again to go out with him and I accepted, and now I am all excited about that. He wants me to go out with him this Saturday night to take me to a show. What do you think?"

"I think that is wonderful. That way you can get to know him a little better," she answered.

"What should I do about Dan?" she asked. "You know, Erika, that he is the first guy I met here in New York, and he turned me on with his affections and I really liked him for that and was beginning to fall in love with him."

"Dan is a very sweet guy. But he has his problems with Jody right now, and I don't think you should get involved. It was a very sad thing that happened to Jody, but it is not a problem that you can solve, and I'm afraid you are just going to get hurt if you stay in there. Dan can handle it, I am sure, and I think that Jody will finally find her way back.

She will just need time and Dan's love."

Darcy looked at Erika and said, "You know what? You are so wise and so right, and I think with this new guy—his name is Brad—I will be eased off from Dan. I'm hoping I will as well as Dan."

Erika got up from her chair and said, "I'm going to bed. I need to get up pretty early as Rod is coming by and pick me up to take me to the police station. They want more information from me about poor Ian."

Both of the girls woke up early the next morning. Darcy had to go to work at the jewelry store, and Erika had to get ready for Rod to pick her up and take her to the police station.

She wasn't looking forward to that. However, she did want them to know about the other man in Ian's life. She hoped that it would help them find the killer.

Before Darcy left, she said to Erika, "Do you think that they will ever find the person who did this?"

"I am sure hoping they will. If I can help them in any way, I will," she said.

Then as Darcy went out the door she said, "I'll see you tonight. Have a good day."

Erika continued to dress and get ready for Rod to pick her up.

As she was waiting, the phone rang. She picked it up and said "Hello."

There was a moment's pause, and then a man with a foreign accent spoke: "Is this Erika Beiler?"

She answered, "Yes"

Then he said, "You had better not get involved or you may get hurt."

Erika quickly asked, "Who is this and what do you mean?" Then the phone went dead.

This really frightened her. What did he mean by that threat she thought? She couldn't wait until Rod got there to pick her up. She had to tell him. She wouldn't know what to do about this without him.

She paced the floor and kept looking out the window to see if he was coming. Soon she saw his red convertible pull up in front, and in a moment, he was on his way upstairs. Thank God, she said to herself. Now she felt a lot better.

In a minute, he was inside her door and grabbed her and kissed her.

Hurrying him, she said, "Let's get into the car Rod, I have something else to tell you."

As they settled inside the car, she said to him, "Rod, I just had a weird phone call, and it scared the wits out of me, and now I don't know what to do."

"Who called you, and what do you mean you don't know what to do?" he asked her.

"Well this person sounded like a man with a foreign accent, and he said I had better not get involved or I may get hurt."

Rod gave her a startled look and said, "That is a threatening call, and we must tell the police. That is something that the police will need to handle. If they think you need protection, then we will make sure you get it," Rod said.

She wanted him to put his arms around her in a protecting sort of way, and she thought that would make everything alright. He seemed so sincere and concerned for her.

When they arrived at the station, he was right next to her going in the door. Rod went up to the counter and said, "We are here to see Sergeant Brady, and this is Erika Beiler."

The officer said, "Just one moment please, and left the counter. Soon he returned and said, "The Sergeant will see you now." and motioned toward the Sergeant's office.So they went into his office, and he asked them to have a seat.

Then he said, "I think you have some information that you believe is important to this case?"

Erika looked over at Rod and started to speak, then Rod interrupted her and said to the Sergeant, "Well, I feel that since I am a witness to what she is going to tell you, perhaps I can explain the whole incident to you."

"Well go ahead," he told Rod.

In minute details, Rod explained the encounter between Ian and this strange man, which occurred in the lobby of the office building that night when they saw them together. He told the officer that to him it seemed as though they were some kind of lovers.

The officer thought a minute and then said, "That sounds interesting, and do you know who this other party was?" He asked both of them.

"No, Erika or I had never seen him before. We were wondering if perhaps Roger might know who he would be but we didn't want to ask him."

"We will check with Roger and see if he can put some light on that incident. Now was there something else you wanted to tell us?" He asked

"As a matter of fact there is something else. Just before we came to see you, Erika received a threatening phone call, which has upset her tremendously," Rod said.

"Well Erika, tell me about this phone call," the officer ordered.

"When I answered the phone, it sounded like a man on the other end with a foreign accent, and he asked, 'Is this Erika Beiler' and I answered, 'Yes.' Then he said, 'You better not get involved or you'll really get hurt.' When he said that, I became very alarmed, and now I worry about my safety."

"I am afraid what they will do if I give any more information. I really don't have too much information about all of this anyway," Erika said.

"Don't you worry about that, you just tell us if there is anything unusual that you think we need to know. We are working on this and have some ideas as to which way to go now, and we will keep an eye on you also."

Then she asked him, "Is it possible for me to get into my studio and continue to work there?"

"I don't see why not. We have done all of the forensic things we need to go ahead with in the case, and I don't see that you would harm anything," he answered her.

She also asked if she could have Betsy and Roger work with her.

"Well now, Betsy is cleared, but we are not sure about Roger as yet, but we hope to be through with him in a few more days after we see if he can shed some light on this other guy or any other guys. Roger has admitted that he and Ian were very intimate, but he seems to have a clear-cut alibi, and we should get that all straightened out very soon. Until then, we cannot release him to work for you." At that moment, Erika felt very sorry for Roger and said she would wait for an answer about clearing the case so she would know if she could use Roger or not. She felt so disappointed she wanted to cry.

At that Rod, reached for her arm and led her out of the office toward his car. As they were walking to the car, he said to her, "I hope that you are feeling a little better now that you got that all straightened out so far."

"Would you care for a little lunch before I go back to work?" he offered.

"If you are up to It, Rod, but do you have the time before going in to your office? I really feel selfish for keeping you away from your work with my problems," she said

"Honey, please don't feel that way; you know I always want to be there for you when you need me," he assured her. Then he asked, "Do you want to go to your studio after we have lunch, or do you want to go home? If you want to go to your studio for awhile, I can come by and pick you up and take you home after I leave the office, OK?"

"You are wonderful Rod," she answered.

He suggested a small lunchroom near the police station, and she said, "That will be fine."

While they were having their lunch, she with a salad and he with a large sandwich, he said to her, "Erika what do you think about going away with me for a few days? I could take a Friday and not go to the office, and we would have Friday, Saturday and Sunday together, and you would not need to think of all these upsetting occurrences?"

She thought awhile and then said, "Thank you, Rod, for asking me and thinking of my welfare that way. You are so sweet to me, but don't forget that I have several high commissioned jobs that I really need to get out before the Christmas holidays. That is why I needed to get back into the studio so that I can work on them. If you can wait 'til I get them completed, then I would really consider that, perhaps during the Christmas holidays, unless you have other plans then."

"I can go anytime that you say, and if you don't think you can go now, maybe we could plan to do something at that time. And if we go during the holidays, I would like to take you home to meet my parents. I am sure they will love you as much as I do," he said to her.

"And just where is your home?" she asked.

"Well my parents have a home in New Salem, New York, which is upper New York State near Albany, where they live most of the time; and they also have a summer home in Hampton, Long Island. I would love to take you to New Salem for the Christmas holidays. I know you would like that. What would you think about that?"

"I will need to think that over and figure out how I can get my Christmas orders out in time. I also may need to take over Ian's orders that he had if the clients would prefer to have me do that," she said to him.

"Well, would you please keep my invitation open, and if you have any idea you might be able to do that, let me know?" She shook her head with an affirming nod.

They finished their lunch, and she said to him, "Rod if you are pressed for time and need to get to the office, I can take a cab home. I really don't mind. I appreciate you giving me your time to go with me to the police station."

"Are you sure you don't mind? I'll get the cab for you, and I'll call you later to make sure you got home alright," he said. He waited until the cab came and gave the cabby the directions and the fare.

When she arrived home, she thought about Jody and wondered how she was getting along. She hadn't inquired from Dan for quite awhile and decided she should go down and see her, but she wanted to call Rod first and let him know she arrived home OK.

She called Rod and told him she arrived home and she would be downstairs talking to Jody for awhile, just in case he tried to call her.

She went downstairs and knocked on Jody's door, but there was no answer. She was pretty sure that Jody would be there as she hadn't been going out since her problem.

Then she called out to Jody, "Jody please, answer your door. It's Erika, and I would like to see you and talk to you, so please open the door will you?"

She waited a couple of minutes, and soon the door opened slowly.

It was Jody, and she looked bedraggled like she had just gotten out of bed. Her hair wasn't combed and no make-up was on though it was late afternoon.

"Hi Jody, how are you feeling? I just got home, and I thought I would stop by and see how you are doing."

As Jody walked over and sat down she asked Erika to have a seat. "I guess I'm alright. I just don't have any ambition or desire to do anything or have anyone around me anymore," she said.

Erika looked at her and wondered if she should say what was in her mind or not, but then again it may do her some good, and if not, it couldn't be any worse than how she is right now.

So she said to her, "Jody I know what you have experienced recently, and I think it was a terrible thing, but you are still alive now, and you must thank God for that. It has been several months now, and you have mended physically, and you are here with all of your friends and most of all with your darling Dan. Everyone loves you and wants you to get back to your old self. They are not blaming you for what happened to you, it was not your fault but just an evil incident that could have happened to any other woman."

She hesitated a few seconds then continued.

"Jody, don't shut everyone out— most of all Dan He loves you, and you are breaking his heart. Open up your heart, and let him in, and you will see that the love you give him and the love he gives to you, will make you better in all ways. I know this is none of my business, but I feel that you are my friend ever since I came here, and it hurts me to see you like this. If my talking to you helps, then I am happy. If you don't appreciate my butting into you problem, then I guess I will just back out of being your friend. Even though I am going through my own big trauma right now, it still bothers me that you will not try harder to come out of this."

There was a long pause, and Erika could see tears flowing down Jody's cheeks

Then she put her arms around Jody and said to her, "I didn't mean to hurt you, Jody, but I like you, and I felt that you just had to have someone convince you that you are still the same sweet person and no different. And I mean no different to anyone who knows you."

Then Jody spoke up and said, "Erika, you are my friend, and I do appreciate all that you have said to me, and what you have said is all true. I will definitely try harder to open up my feelings to everyone and most of all to my sweet husband, Dan. I realize now what he has been going through with me and I really don't want to see things go on like this for him any longer. You will see I have, as of now, made up my mind to get out of this rut."

Erika put her arms around her and gave her a little kiss on her salty cheek. Then she said "I do hope you try, Jody, and I'll see you later." Then Erika went out the door.

When she got into her apartment, Darcy was there, and Erika told her all that she told Jody. Then she said to Darcy, "I think she will start to get herself out of her rut. Anyway, that's what she said she would do. I really gave her something to think about and maybe she will listen to me or maybe not. We will just have to wait and see."

She told Darcy everything that happened to her on this day and how wonderful Rod was to help her the way he did. Darcy listened intently and agreed that Rod was a prince of a guy, and Erika should make a decision that he is the one for her.

Erika wanted to change the subject and asked her how her day was and if she had seen her friend, Brad.

"As a matter of fact, I spoke to the boss about him and asked her what she thought and she told me that she had known him for a long time and thought he was a nice guy, and he certainly was safe to go out with. Later he did come into the store, and we had quite a long talk.

And you know what Erika? The more I talked to him, the more I liked him.

He asked me if I had decided to accept his invitation to the movies some night. He still wants to take me out. So I accepted the invite."

"When are you going out with him?" Erika asked.

"He would like to go out Saturday." she said. "I told him that was fine with me, so I am sure we will go to the movies Saturday night.

Then looking at Erika, she said, "Now what's with you? How is everything going at the studio, and did they find out who killed your boss, Ian?"

"No they haven't decided definitely, but they have their suspicions, and I guess it won't be long now. Poor Ian, I miss him. I have asked to get back into the studio to do my work, and they said it was OK, but I won't have Roger to help me unless they can clear him out as a suspect. But I can have Betsy, and that will help."

Erika told Darcy that she was going to prepare some chicken pies for their dinner and asked if that sounded OK with her. Since neither one of them had any plans for the night, Darcy said, "That sounds good, and I'll make a salad." They both agreed to have dinner and retire early. They had their dinner and were cleaning up the kitchen when there was a loud knock on the door. Remembering the warning that Darcy gave, she called out and said, "Who's there?"

The answer came back, "It's Dan Erika, I want to tell you something." Darcy opened the door and Dan came in. As the girls were ready to listen to what he had to tell them, he went on. "I wanted to let you know that I just learned from the police that they located the two guys who did all that to Jody. They have had tails on them for some time but couldn't quite nail them. It seems that they have had trouble before, and our police here got some finger prints out of Jody's car, and they matched the prints of both of them. I asked the police why they didn't get them right away, and they said the guys were from New Jersey, and they had a hard time tracking them. They are having them extradited back to New York. I'm sure glad they found them, and I hope they lock them up for a very long time."

"I sure hope so too, Dan," Darcy said to him.

"By the way, Erika, Jody told me about your little talk today, and she said it really made her feel more alive. I want to thank you for that, I think it will make a big difference in our relationship, so thanks again. I really appreciate what you do. Thank you also, Darcy, for holding my hand through my bad times. It really did help, and I appreciated that."

"Erika, I also wanted to give you my condolences in behalf of what you are going through at your work. That's another tragedy to endure right now. Have they discovered who did it yet?" Dan asked.

Erika said, "No they haven't. They have been asking me for any help that I can give them, but I haven't the slightest idea who would want to kill Ian. He was a dear man, and I sure do miss him and the help he gave to me in my work. They have a few clues, but they are not saying much about them. They know that he had several male lovers, but they don't know just who they all are, and they don't know, as yet, if it was a love triangle or a business disagreement. I'm sure they will solve it soon."

"Well I won't keep you gals any longer. I'm sure you are both tired, but I wanted to let you in on the latest that I knew," he said, bidding them goodnight.

"Thank you," they both chimed in, "for the information, Dan." Then they all said goodnight.

Erika and Darcy looked at each other, and Darcy said to Erika, "Gosh, I'm sure glad that they found those guys, and I'm sure they will be prosecuted for what they have done."

"I certainly hope so," Erika agreed

"Now all they need to do is to find who is responsible for Ian's death. That seems to be a big puzzle for them. Do you know what I think, Darcy?" Erika said to her. "I think Ian had someone we don't know about that he had a relationship with, and there was a lot of jealousy involved. He was involved with Roger, and there is that other man that Rod and I saw him with that night, and there could be someone else in the picture also. Who can tell how many he had? They have a lot of investigating to do."

"Well, I'm ready to hit the hay. As they say at home, tomorrow is another day," Darcy said. So they both retired to their bedrooms. Erika laid thinking about continuing her business at the studio, and how to improve it.

As she thought about it, an idea came to her. What if she could design her own fabrics? "I would design my own patterns on the fabrics, and they would be exclusive fabric available to only me," she said to herself. The more she thought about that, the more enthused she became. Then she would have something that no one else would have. What would she need to do in order to do that, she thought? She decided to look into it as soon as she could. She couldn't remember falling asleep after that.

They both rose very early. Erika wanted to get to the studio and check to see what she would need to do to continue with their orders, both hers and Ian's.

When she arrived at the studio, Betsy was there but not Roger. She decided that since they were alone she would have a long talk with Betsy and see just how much she knew about Ian.

She beckoned to Betsy to follow her and sit at one of the large tables where she thought they would not be disturbed. She said to Betsy, "Good morning, Betsy. How are you today? You look a little tired, have you been getting any sleep lately?"

"Well, the first few nights after that happened to Ian I couldn't sleep, but last night I did get a few hours," she said. "The thing that bothers me the most is what is happening with Roger. He could not have hurt Ian. He thought too much of him, and I know Roger meant the world to Ian. I think that there is someone else who knew that and was jealous and couldn't handle Ian's rejections," Betsy said to Erika with tears in her eyes.

Then Erika asked her, "Are you in love with Roger?"

"No Erika, I really like him and have known him a long time, but I am not in love with him. But I hate to see him get hurt."

"Betsy, do you know of any other man who may have had designs on Ian's feelings?" Erika asked her.

"Not that I can think of right this minute," Betsy answered.

"I'll tell you something, Betsy. One night when my friend Rod and I were coming in to the studio, we ran into Ian and some other man, and they were real cozy together, and Rod and I instantly surmised that they had something going together. When they saw us they separated, and when we came back out, they were gone. The other man was taller than Ian and heavier and looked like he was from another country. He wore a light grey overcoat. Would you have any idea who that man could have been?"

Betsy thought a minute and then said, "Gosh Erika, there are so many men that come into the studio, like all the suppliers' representatives, and I very seldom pay any attention to them. Maybe if I go over all of them and analyze each one I might be able to answer that for you."

"Betsy, if you can come up with anything, it might help Roger. So please try for him and Ian. Please, please try hard to think of something or someone. We need Roger back here.

Then as they began to talk about their work, Erika told Betsy about the idea she had for making her own patterns on the fabric. Betsy's eyes lit up, and she agreed that it was a very good idea. She also informed Erika that she knew one of the fabric representatives who she was sure could help Erika expedite her idea, and she would give his information to Erika. Erika thanked her and excused her to go back to her work.

Erika proceeded to go over the orders that she had and also the ones that Ian had. She knew she would need to contact Ian's clients to ask them if they would like to continue with her to complete their orders or if they would prefer to take the orders elsewhere.

She contacted them by phone, and after hearing about Ian's death, they were all very sorry, but every one of them decided to stay with her to complete their orders. She felt good about that but knew she would need to get more help in order to handle all of the orders.

Later, Betsy came in and informed her that the fabric salesman she had suggested to her was going to be in the next day, and Erika could talk to him about her special fabrics.

After taking care of the technical questions, Erika organized her office to comply with her systems, since Ian was no longer there. Then she decided she had a busy day and would call it a day and go home.

When she reached the apartment and was just going into the building, she met Greg going in. She was surprised to see him. He looked as sharp as ever.

"Oh hi, Erika," he greeted her.

"How are you, Greg?' she asked.

"I'm fine, how are you doing? I haven't seen you for quite awhile. You must be very busy with your work," he said

"Yes, I have been. You have heard about Ian, the owner of my studio haven't you?" she asked.

"Yes, I read about it. That must make things pretty difficult for you, huh?" he said.

"Oh it has, but the worst part is they haven't found who did this awful thing yet, and it keeps everything in an uproar until they do," she told him.

"Well I sure hope things ease up for you soon. You don't deserve this."

"Thank you, Greg. You are a sweet man," she said to him as he looked into her eyes with his beautiful blue eyes, and again she got that tingle,

"I hope that I get to see you over the holidays. Do you think that will be possible?" he asked.

"I can't see any reason why not, but you must realize that before the holidays I am very busy at the studio."

"I do understand that, but could I just call and check on you occasionally?" he asked in his sweet way.

"Yes, of course, Greg," she answered.

He put his arm around her and gave her a tight hug, and they bid each other goodnight.

Erika continued to her apartment, and when she entered, she called out to see if Darcy had gotten home before her, but there was no answer. She went to the refrigerator to see if there was something she could snack on because she didn't feel up to cooking anything for herself. She was tired tonight as her days lately had been very stressful for her. After she had eaten some left-over pizza, she decided to retire for the night.

She had just fallen asleep when the phone rang and awakened her. She jumped out of bed and took the phone and said, "Hello." There was no answer, so she said, "Hello, Hello," but still no answer.

Finally, she heard the same voice she had heard with the previous phone warning: "You better keep your nose out of this, or you're going to get hurt. This is my last warning," he said to her.

"Who is this?" she asked. "Who is calling?" Then he hung up the phone.

When she had gotten back in bed, she lay awake thinking what she should do. She thought the best thing to do would be to go to the police and tell them what was happening. So she decided she would go to the police the next morning as soon as she got up. She didn't hear Darcy when she came in very late, as she had fallen asleep.

The next morning when she awoke, she told Darcy what had happened, and Darcy agreed that she should go to the police and this time ask them if they could put a tracer on her incoming phone calls, just in case he called again. Erika agreed that was a good idea. But he had told her that this was his last warning, and what if he didn't call her back, Erika thought. She would contact the police this morning nevertheless.

After dressing, she called the sergeant and told him what had happened and asked him if he could put a tracer on the calls. Then he told her that they already had her phone lines tapped, and they knew who was doing the calling. He said they would be making an arrest very shortly, and when they did, he would inform her who it was. Then they would bring him in for questioning about the murder of Ian.

She told him she was afraid for her safety and fearful of going to the studio. Then he said, "Don't worry, Miss Beiler. We have had you watched from the time you received the first warning. I don't think he will come near you if he knows you are being protected by us."

She said, "Thank you sergeant," and hung up the phone.

Erika was glad she had called the sergeant and felt a little better but couldn't wait until they arrested this person.

She continued to prepare to go to the studio and had a little chat with Darcy before taking off. She told Darcy what the sergeant had told her about being protected, and Darcy said she was glad to hear that.

Darcy told her that she had a date with Brad that night, and she wouldn't be home 'til late.

Erika said, "That's great, Darcy, do you like this guy?"

Darcy smiled in sort of a sheepish way and answered, "Yes, I think I like him very much, but I'm not making any rash decisions yet. We'll see after I see him a few times." With that, she went out the door to work.

Before Erika left, she decided to call Rod and relate to him what the sergeant had told her. Rod said that he was certainly happy to hear that because he was worrying about the same thing happening, that she was concerned about.

Then he asked her if she had been considering his offer to go with him over the holidays to spend a few days with his parents.

Erika was silent for a moment, mulling it over in her mind.

And then Rod said, "Erika, did you hear my question?"

Finally she answered and said, "I would like very much to go with you and wondered if your parents are going to chaperone us, or are you planning on us being alone?"

"By all means, my parents are going to be there. I always spend Christmas with them, and I would be overjoyed to have you join me with my family. You will be absolutely safe, and they will welcome you, and I know that they will love you as much as I do.

You and I will have a lot of fun being there together. I am sincerely hoping you will accept my invitation."

"Rod, I will accept your invitation, but I must get all of my work at the studio caught up before I can leave. There are only four weeks until the holidays are here. Can you tell me just when you would like go so that I can plan my work schedule? It is important that I know what jobs I need to complete before I can leave."

"I am looking to stay up there for at least four or five days. That will give you three weeks to finish up your commitments. Does that sound like it is enough time for your work?" he asked.

"I'm hoping I can work that in. I know I could if I had Roger back in the studio," she said.

The thought of going away alone with Rod gave her a thrill. She really liked Rod, but could never feel that she really was in love with him. Was she just holding back her love for him? It seemed that she couldn't do anything without him.

Would it make a difference when she was alone in a new place with him? She always felt secure with him, and sometimes she would get a thrill out of his advances, but never had that tingle feeling like she did with Greg. But then Rod never got really amorous with her as Greg did. Well, maybe when she spends four days with him, she will know something.

Finally, she went out the door and headed for the studio, as it was getting late, and she wanted to check on the work that Betsy was doing. She was working on a design for an important client.

If she really wanted to go with Rod, she would need to get on the ball and finish some of her jobs plus the jobs that Ian was commissioned to do

Just as she entered the studio, Betsy told her that she was wanted on the phone. Erika was a little apprehensive in taking the call, remembering the strange man's warning.

Taking the phone from Betsy, she said, "This is Erika."

The voice said, "Erika, this is Sergeant Brady at the police department. I just wanted to inform you that we have found the man that we suspect is the killer of your boss, Ian. We are very sure that he is the man that you and your friend saw in the lobby with Ian. When he thought we were getting close to him, he took his own life and left a note regarding his jealousy and his involvement with Ian. When you come down to the station, I will give you a complete report about the case."

Thank you, Sergeant, for the information. Now what about Roger, is he exonerated? And is he permitted to come back to work for me?" she asked.

"Yes, he has been cleared and is being released today."

"Oh, thank you again, Sergeant," She replied.

Going to her drawing board, she decided that as soon as she could she would go see the sergeant and get the full details about the case from him. She wanted to wait and see if Roger would come in today. She hoped he would because she could sure use his help.

In the meantime, she returned to her work on the designs that she was working on and waited for the fabric salesman to come in.

While she was waiting, her thoughts were of Rod and his invitation to go away with him. It sort of excited her to think of that. What were his parents like? And how would they accept her? Would she have the proper clothes to take with her? Maybe she had better design a few new items to take. She would need to have them made up in a hurry now as time was getting close

Rod said it was snowing up there now, so she had better design something to wear in the snow that would keep her warm—something like a snow suit. She had some good ideas for winter weather attire and hoped she could get them worked out. She could do that now if Roger was coming back to help her.

She went to Betsy and told her what the sergeant had said, and that Roger was exonerated, and Betsy was so pleased that tears came to her eyes.

Soon the fabric salesman came in, and after talking to him, she became more pleased about her plan. He said he could supply her with very elegant fabrics that would include beaded fabrics and laces and fabrics with tiny pearls, crystals, gemstones, gold and various priceless items woven into some of them He also had a source for her to obtain fabrics with her own design woven into it.

Now she was sure that she could offer one-of-a-kind designs to her clients. She was very elated about her new plan and couldn't wait to start on it.

After talking to the salesman a little longer and giving him her order, she decided to call Roger and see if he was coming in the next day. She obtained the phone number from Betsy and called him.

When he answered he said, "Hello, this is Roger," and Erika told him how pleased she was that he was freed and was looking forward to him being in the studio the next morning.

"You are planning on coming back to work here aren't you, Roger?" she asked.

"Oh yes, I would like to. Are you going to be continuing with the same operation?" he asked.

"Yes, I have spoken to all of Ian's clients, and they were sorry to hear about Ian, but they still would like to continue with us. So, I really need you, Roger, as we have several commitments to get out before the holidays," she pleaded

"Well, I will be there and happy that you still want me, Erika," he assured her.

"Good, Roger, then I will see you in the morning."

After talking to Roger, she began to think about the new fabrics she had just ordered and would be getting in. She decided right then that she would have her personal fashion show and have her own runway showing her latest designs with her new fabrics. She decided to begin on that project right away.

She thought of Rod and wanted to call him and let him know what the sergeant had told her about the man who killed Ian. So she dialed his number and his secretary answered with "Rod Burton's office." And Erika asked to please speak with Mr. Burton. The secretary said, "One moment please."

Soon Rod's voice said, "This is Rod Burton, may I help you?"

"Hi Rod, this is Erika, and I just wanted to tell you that they found the man who they are sure killed Ian. It was the man that you and I saw in the lobby that night. I understand that he left a note confessing everything and told the whole story, after that he took his own life. I am going down to the station tomorrow morning and the sergeant said he would give me all of the details then. I can tell you more about it when I get all the information."

"I'm sure glad that is all over for your sake, Erika," he said.

"I am too," she agreed. "I'm sorry to bother you, and I'll talk to you later. I have some questions to ask you about the trip to your home for the holidays," she said.

"OK, I'll call you later," he said.

Her mind went back to planning a new wardrobe for her trip. She drew up some things that she thought would be appropriate and warm and still very attractive. Her first thought was for a very warm outfit, so she drew up one consisting of beige wool pants with fitted legs and a red turtle neck sweater with a finger- tip length jacket in the same beige material, trimmed with white, faux-fox fur collar and cuffs. She decided that she would wear beige boots with this outfit.

For a formal occasion she designed a long gown made of cranberry colored velvet with sleeves just below the elbow and attached at the bodice to bare the shoulders. The bodice was fitted, and silver, metallic braids accented the underwire bra line, and the skirt flowed full from the hips. To accompany this, she had a matching shawl for warmth, which contained designs on each end with the silver braids and cranberry colored fringe on the edges.

Another outfit she was making was a dinner or cocktail dress that was quite formal. It was to be made in black peau de soie fabric with an ankle length straight line skirt having a slit that opened from the knee to the bottom of the hem line on one side. It was strapless and had a fitted bodice with braided lame outlining an underwire design. To be worn with it was a short, black lace jacket with sleeves that flared just above the wrist.

She knew she would design a couple more, but they would just be very simple. Also, she would go shopping to purchase some additional things to wear in the snow. Going with Rod was a few weeks away, but as time went on, she became more anxious. So she made up her mind to knuckle down and get her orders out and make up her own wardrobe.

By the time she left the studio for the day she was really tired. She was looking forward to Roger returning to the studio; it would be a great relief for her.

When she arrived at home, Darcy was there and had a big salad all ready for the two of them.

Erika said to her, "I am so glad you did this Darcy, as I was thinking I would just go to bed without eating because I'm too tired to even think about preparing anything."

Then she asked Darcy, "How was your day?"

"My day was great. I'm selling more each day and now with the holidays, things are getting very good. People are buying more jewelry."

"That's great. And how were your dates with Brad? Do you still like him?"

"Yes I do. I like him very much. In fact, he wants me to go away with him for the Christmas holidays to the Pocono Mountains for four days to play in the snow. I told him I would consider it. What do you think?"

"Well, if you think you like him well enough to be alone with him for four days, I think that would be fun," Erika advised her.

"As a matter of fact, I'm glad to hear that because Rod has asked me to go to his folks place up north for the holidays, and I was a little apprehensive about leaving you alone for the holidays. We will be staying with his folks so I thought it should be alright. And now that I'm making a special wardrobe for up there, I'm getting excited about the trip," she said.

"Gee, that sounds great, Erika. Do you think Rod is getting real serious?" Darcy asked.

"Gosh, I don't know what to think. Sometimes I think he is, like when he wants me to make a commitment to him," she told her.

As they ate their salads, Erika said to Darcy, "Wow, this is a delicious salad; we should have this more often. It would be good for us and healthy." Darcy agreed with her.

Then she repeated the news to Darcy that she had gotten from the sergeant at the police station, that the man had killed himself after leaving a note about the situation. She told Darcy that she was going down to the station in the morning and the sergeant would give her all the details.

"I'm sure glad that is solved. Maybe you can get it off your mind and start fresh. Let me know what the sergeant tells you, will you?"

"Sure I will. But as soon as I help you clean up our dinner, I'm going to bed and I'll see you in the morning. Goodnight." Then off to the shower and bed she went. In no time she had fallen asleep and was dreaming about this adventure that she had coming up in a couple of weeks.

She dreamed of them frolicking in the snow. He was chasing her up a hill, and she couldn't run very fast in the snow, and soon he caught her, and they both fell into a snow-drift. He grabbed her and hugged her; then she felt his hot lips on hers and tried to fight him off. She kept yelling, "Let me go Rod." And it seemed that he didn't hear her so she got louder and louder: "Rod let me go! Let me go! Let me go!"

"Rod, Let me go!!" Suddenly she felt someone shaking her, and she woke up and saw Darcy and wondered what she was doing there.

"Erika, you were yelling so loud about someone letting you go, and I couldn't wake you. I guess you were having a nightmare," Darcy said.

"Oh yes, I was having a dream about Rod and I in the snow up there where we are going. I guess I must have been too tired tonight. Thanks, Darcy, and hope I didn't disturb your sleep."

"No, that's OK, I wasn't fully asleep yet." Saying goodnight again, Darcy went off to her room.

The next morning Erika arose, and after showering and dressing, she headed for the police station and the talk with the sergeant.

He greeted her and asked her into his office and to have a seat. "Well, I guess you are pretty relieved to hear the news, huh?" he asked.

"Very much so," she answered, "for many reasons. I'm glad it's over, and I'm happy Roger can come back to work for me. Now you said you would give me all of the details, can you do that?"

"Yes, I will. To start with, we found out that Ian and this man, Keith, had been living together for some time and then Keith moved out. No one knew that they had lived together except Roger; and Roger was Ian's companion before this Keith.

Roger says that he never lived with Ian but they were very fond of one another, and he knew that Ian asked Keith to move out, which he did.

It seems that Ian found another lover and wanted his new lover to move in with him, and when this Keith found out about the plan, he became very irate, and they argued a lot, and we discovered that many people saw them argue. When Ian told him that he was going to have his new lover move in with him, no matter if Keith approved it or not, Keith became very angry. He really saw red and decided to kill Ian so no one else could have him.

He went to the studio after everyone had left for the day. He and Ian got into a big fight, and he decided he didn't want anyone to know that he had been kicked out by Ian. He said in his note that he loved Ian for a very long time and thought that they were made for each other, and he wasn't happy not living with Ian. He couldn't bear to see him living with anyone else. He decided no one else was going to have Ian, so during their argument he just pulled out his gun and he shot him. When he discovered that Ian was dead he realized he couldn't be with Ian any longer, he just wanted to die also.

"We had your phone tapped since he gave you the warning on the first call he made to you. We located where he was calling from and had a tail on him for quite some time. He knew we were getting close, and it wouldn't be long before we caught up with him, so he decided to end it all himself. He wrote in his note that he didn't want to live without Ian anyway. The investigators thought that perhaps Roger had something to do with the killing. That is why we had to hold him for awhile, and we also thought he could shed some light on the investigation to help us. He knew of this Keith but didn't know him personally. He did give us a lot of help because he was Ian's lover previously, but we had evidence that it ended some time ago for him. So that is the full story, and I'm sure you are happy it's all over."

"Thank you, sergeant. Yes, I am very happy but still feel sorry for poor Ian; I will surely miss him," she said.

"I know how you feel but life must go on and I wish you all the luck with your new venture. I'm sure you will do fine even without Ian. You are a very determined person."

She thanked him again and bid him a good day.

When she arrived at the studio, Roger was there and after welcoming him back and telling him how much she missed his help, she gave him some instructions to proceed with one of the orders that she wanted to complete for Ian's client. It was a very elaborate gown with lots of metallic embroidery on some very fine silk, and he was very meticulous about that type of work, so she wanted him to work on it.

She went to work on her personal things. She wanted to get them done so she would have an idea if she needed more or not. She would discuss that with Rod to see what he thought.

The work load was going to be very heavy for the next two weeks, getting out all the orders she had as well as the ones that Ian had. She didn't take time for any socializing. She was dragging by the end of the day.

Darcy was getting worried that Erika was overdoing it and told her that.

"Oh I'm OK. I'll get through this, and I will be able to rest when I go with Rod," she told Darcy.

"Oh no, that's what you think. Rod will keep you busy," Darcy said.

Erika smiled at Darcy and said, "Do you really think so?"

Then Erika asked Darcy, "Did you give Brad your final decision about going away with him for the four days, and where did you say he wanted to take you?"

"Yes, I told him that I would love to go. He wants to go to the Poconos and teach me some skiing. He loves to ski, and I never have done that and don't know how. He thinks it will be fun, so I accepted his invitation."

Erika said to her, "I never did go skiing either and don't know how.

I wonder if Rod will want to ski when we go up there. I don't know if I can learn now; maybe I'm too clumsy and my legs too long," Erika said. Then they both laughed out loud.

"We are not getting any younger, so we better learn what we don't know as soon as we can," Darcy said, and they both burst out laughing again.

Just then the phone rang, and Darcy picked it up. She handed it to Erika and said, "It's for you. It sounds like Rod."

"This is Erika," she said.

"Hi there, how are you doing? Remember when I asked if I could see you before the holidays, and you said you would see if it would not interfere with your work?"

Yes, Greg, I remember," She answered.

"Well, I'm going home for the holidays, and I would really like to see you before I go. I will be leaving sometime in the next week. Do you think you could break away one night next week before I go?"

She asked, "What night were you thinking of, Greg? I could possibly make it this Saturday if that sounds alright with you."

"That sounds great. Let's make it Saturday then. I'll call you before that to confirm it if you don't mind."

"No, that's fine Greg. I'll talk to you then. Bye." Then she hung up.

"Wow, what was that all about? I thought it was Rod on the other end. Are you still seeing Greg also? What's Rod going to think about that?"

"Well, Greg asked me some time ago if he could see me before the holidays, and I told him, yes, if I wasn't going to be too busy. He sort of pleaded with me, and I asked him to call me later, and this is later, I guess. So I will see him Saturday. I haven't seen him for quite awhile," Erika said.

"Both of those guys are serious about you, and I think you will have to make up your mind very shortly as to which one you are in love with and which one is important in your life," Darcy told her.

Erika just looked at her and didn't know what to say to that remark, so she just dropped it.

Today was Saturday, and when Erika awoke and looked out the window, she saw that it was snowing. It was such a pretty sight to see everything covered with the white snow, but the sun was coming out, and she thought it wouldn't be long until the snow would be gone if it wasn't cold enough to stick.

Then she remembered that tonight was the night she was going to see Greg. What should she wear? It would need to be something warm. Well, she had a nice warm wool skirt that she made from fabric that came from Ireland. It was very pretty—shamrock green—and the sweater that would go well with it would be her turtleneck cashmere with a printed pattern with many colors of red, green and gold and lots of sparkles woven into it. It zipped from the top of the neck line to the bottom with sparkles edging the zipper on each side. She thought that would be warm enough for her with a colorful scarf. She would wear her coat that she had just made for herself and the hat that she made to match—a skull-type trimmed with the same faux-fur and two little fur balls hanging down on one side and her beige boots and handbag. She decided the outfit would look festive enough to be with Greg for the holidays.

Having decided all of that, she stood by the window looking out at the people and the cars going by covered with snow. She thought it was such a beautiful picture. Then she wondered if it would be like that where she was going with Rod.

Then she had the thought that she must send something to her family for Christmas, she began to think. What would they appreciate she wondered. Then she decided to write to her sister, Rachel, and see what she would suggest.

She sat down and wrote Rachel a letter and asked her to please let her know soon, as she would be gone for the holidays, which was only about ten days away. She got the letter into the mail as soon as she finished it.

Spending the rest of the day chatting with Darcy about her dates with Brad and spending time on her vanity, Erika found that she was getting a little excited about seeing Greg.

She was just getting ready to get into the shower when the phone rang. She picked it up in her bedroom and said, "Hello."

"Hi there, what are you doing?" Rod asked.

"I was just getting into the shower and getting ready to go out," she answered.

"Oh, I was thinking that maybe you and I could go out someplace tonight for dinner, but if you have other plans, I guess we will need to postpone it, don't you think?"

"Yes, Rod, I am sorry but I have other plans for tonight, so we will need to postpone it."

By the way, Rod, you didn't say what day we would be leaving here and if you are driving. How are we traveling?"

"Yes, sweetie, I am driving, and it should be OK as I will keep in touch with the highway department to make sure the highways are clear. Don't you worry, OK? We should leave here a week from today. I can't wait to get you alone so I can take you in my arms," he said in a very sweet way. "Is that going to fit in with your work schedule?" He asked.

"It will be fine," she answered.

"Erika, I can hardly wait for next week to get here. We will have a great time together, and we will play in the snow, and maybe if you are willing, I will teach you to ski. Would you like that?" he asked.

"Oh, that will be fun. Darcy is going away for four days with her friend to the Poconos, and he is going to teach her to ski, and she is anxious to learn," she told him.

"Great!" He exclaimed.

Then she said, "Rod, I must say goodnight. I need to get ready to go out, and I'll talk to you tomorrow."

OK, my sweet. I'll call you tomorrow. Goodnight," He said, and they both hung up.

When she was completely ready, she looked at herself in the full-view mirror and was pleased at how her attire looked on her.

Darcy came in and made the remark that she looked great, and was she so sure she wasn't trying to win over Greg more than he was already?

"No, that is not my idea, but I wanted to look good for Greg because he is so sweet and patient with me, and because I'm being with him before he leaves for the holidays. I thought it would be a nice send-off for him."

"I see," Darcy said with a grin. "Anyway, you have a great evening with Greg tonight. You deserve it; you've been working pretty hard."

Erika thanked her, and just then there came a knock on the door, and she went to answer it.

She opened the door, and there stood Greg. He looked so handsome in his grey pants, dark blue jacket and red tie. He had a red and green plaid scarf around his neck and was carrying a dark blue trench coat.

He asked her, "Are you ready, Erika?" and she confirmed that she was.

So after saying goodnight to Darcy, they descended the stairway and out to the car.

When they entered the car, he asked, "Do you care for Italian food?"

"Oh yes I do," she answered

"Well, I thought I would take you to this nice Italian restaurant where they have a little entertainment and nice cozy, secluded booths where we can have a small amount of privacy. Does that sound alright with you?"

"Perfect," she agreed.

As they drove on, he pulled her over close to him, as he had done before when she was with him in the car. "You look absolutely ravishing tonight, Erika, and more beautiful every time I see you." And he reached over and kissed her on her cheek. She felt the heat of his lips, and it was warming to her.

They reached the restaurant and after entering, the Maitre d' ushered them to the booth that Greg requested. Greg took her coat and scarf and hung them on the appropriate hook, along with his. He asked Erika if she would like a cocktail and she said she would take whatever he was having. So, he ordered a bottle of imported wine. When the waiter brought it, he poured a small amount for Greg to approve, and after Greg approved it, he served them both.

Greg asked her if she had something that she preferred for her Entre' and she said, "I'll have what you are ordering, please." So he ordered for both of them. It was something parmesan. She didn't know what it was but decided she would just be surprised. Then he made a toast to her with the wine saying something sweet, and they clicked their glasses.

As she sipped the wine, it was very warm going down, and after two glasses, she was hoping the waiter would serve them soon as Greg was refilling her glass along with his.

They talked about her work and the Ian murder case and Jody's case. They also got onto the subject of Erika's business. She told him about the great new fabrics that she was getting in and what she wanted to do with them. Greg was keeping her wine glass full and she was beginning to feel light-headed and all warm inside.

Soon the waiter served them, and the dinner was delicious, with more wine. It seemed as though they were there for hours talking, but it was actually only a little over two hours.

Then Greg asked, "Honey, are you ready to leave?"

And Erika said, "I think so, or I won't be able to walk out on my own."

He said, "That's OK, Honey, then I can carry you and hold you closer to me." He squeezed her around the waist and helped her with her coat and scarf.

On the way home, he said to her, "Erika, do you know how much I care for you?"

"Well I think you like me or you wouldn't ask me out, and I like you or I wouldn't accept your invitations. Does that answer your question?"

"You are so clever, Miss Beiler," he said as he kissed her on the cheek again. It was getting very cold, and he hugged her close to him and kissed her again, and that very warm kiss gave her a tingle that seemed to warm her all the way down.

When they reached the apartment building, he drove the car to his underground parking space, and they had to walk up the back way to the apartment. They approached his apartment first, and he asked her to come in for awhile, and he would thaw them out with a fire in the fireplace, and make her a good hot toddy drink. Oh, that sounded good to Erika, and she consented.

When they reached his apartment, they entered, and Greg removed her coat and scarf and lit the fireplace. Then Greg went into the kitchen to make the drinks. Erika was enjoying the fireplace, watching the flames, and soon he came back with their drinks. He set them down on the coffee table and came around to her on the sofa and sat next to her, and they sipped their drinks and talked about the date that they just had together. The drinks were very warm going down and the heat from the fireplace and the heat of the drinks made her more lightheaded.

During their conversation, he put his arms around her and looked directly into her eyes and she peered into his, and then it happened— she was drowning in those beautiful blue eyes going down, down, down; she didn't care where. He was kissing her passionately and his hot lips traveled all over her face and neck, then he unzipped the sweater that she was wearing and continued to slowly remove it with his arms around her. He reclined her body on the sofa and began to kiss her all over, first his hot lips were on her eyes then found her lips for a long passionate kiss, then down to her neck He kept going until he found her breasts. Now she was in ecstasy and wanted to have more. She was oblivious of the world outside of the two of them, and finally he pressed his hot lips on hers again.

She was all shaky inside and tears started to roll down her cheeks. He felt the wetness of her tears on her cheeks.

"Darling, please don't cry. I didn't mean to make you cry," he said.

"No, Greg, I don't know what came over me, to accept your caresses so readily. I never intended for this to happen," she said as she was adjusting her sweater.

"I'm happy it happened," he said. "Now I know how you feel about me. You are wonderful, and I am in love with you, Erika."

"I'm going to miss you while I am gone for the holidays, but there is one thing I would like you to do for me when I get back, if you will," he said.

"What is that, Greg?" she asked.

"I am thinking about buying an apartment in Manhattan, and I would like you to go with me to see it and give me your opinion on it. Would you do that for me?" he asked.

"Yes, I will, Greg, but why do you need my opinion? If you like it, then that's all that is important, right?" She said.

"It is very important that you like it, as I expect you to be there most of the time after I move in," he said to her.

"That is very thoughtful of you, Greg, and I'll be happy to go with you and give you my opinion."

"Well, I'll call you when I get back and see if you will go because I would like very much to have your approval on it before I make the deal, OK?" he asked

"Thank you for the confidence in my taste," she said.

"Now I will walk you up to your apartment," he said, hugging her tightly and kissing her eyes, nose, cheeks and then her lips with his very hot lips. He led her out the door to the stairs.

When they got to her apartment, it was another embrace and many hot kisses on the lips. Then he thanked her for an unforgettable night and said he hoped they could repeat it very soon. It seemed as though he wanted to hang on to her and not let her go.

Finally, she said, "Greg I must go in now. Thank you for the evening. It was wonderful, and I wish you a very Merry Christmas. I will see you when you get back after the holidays. "

He said "OK," and departed.

It was very hard for her to fall asleep that night. All she could think about was the time she had with Greg. Would she always have that on her mind or would she be able to forget it? It was a feeling that she had never experienced before, and it was wonderful, but was he the one she really wanted? She asked herself.

She noticed that Darcy hadn't come in yet, so she went right to bed. She was almost asleep when she heard Darcy come in, and then she went back to sleep.

The next thing she knew, the sun was pouring in her room, and it looked like a beautiful day. She heard Darcy moving around in her room, so decided she would get up and prepare a little breakfast for them both. Darcy soon came out to the kitchen area and pitched in to help.

"Wow, this is a beautiful day even if the snow is still out there. It makes the sun seem so much brighter reflecting on the white snow. I wish we had something exciting to do today, don't you? Darcy asked.

"Was Brad going to be busy today? Erika asked.

"Well, since the holidays are getting so close, the stores are getting busy and they need more merchandise, so he had a few calls to make today, and he said he would call me later. What about you?" she asked.

"I haven't heard from Rod yet. He did call just before I went out last night but didn't say anything about today. I don't mind though, because I need a little time to myself today," she answered.

"Oh and by the way, how was your date with Greg last night? Surely he told you how great you looked?" Darcy inquired.

"Yes, he did that and we had a delightful, romantic Italian dinner and then went back to his place and spent the rest of the evening sitting by the fire drinking hot toddies and making love, and it was wonderful." She responded

"No wonder you need a little time to yourself today," Darcy said to her with a smile.

"After the holidays, Greg wants me to go with him to give my opinion on an apartment he wants to buy in Manhattan, and I told him I would."

"That's nice. Is he thinking about having you move in with him?" Darcy asked.

"I don't believe so, but I would not consider that anyway. I wish he hadn't come on so strong with me. I really had more considering to do before that would happen, and I am just getting ready to go away with Rod," she said to Darcy.

"Well, you know what Erika? A person's heart is their guide, and there comes a time when your heart just does what it wants to do. I think he is so crazy about you, and he just let his heart be his guide," Darcy told her.

"Well, he is a sweet person, and I do like him a lot, but I am still not sure. I know it must be either Greg or Rod, but then I have met very few men since I came here so how can I be sure?"

A little later that morning Greg called her and asked how she was feeling. She told him she was feeling fine. He thanked her again for last night and told her he was still feeling her in his arms and now he wishes he wasn't going away as he needed to be close to her. She told him it might be good for him to be away for awhile anyway. He said again that he was going to miss her and he would talk to her again before he left.

During the morning Erika and Darcy chatted more about their affairs and then the phone rang, and Darcy picked it up.

She handed it to Erika and said, "I'm sorry, I thought it might be Brad, but it is Rod."

"Hi, this is Erika."

"Hi, Pumpkin," he greeted her, calling her that for the first time. "How are you today? It is such a beautiful day, I thought I would like to take you for a drive and talk about our trip, and you could question me about all the things you would like to know concerning the trip. Would you agree?"

"That sounds fine. You will need to give me time to freshen up and dress as I have just been lying around here doing nothing."

"Would an hour give you enough time?" he asked

"That would be fine," she answered

"I'll see you in an hour," he said, and they hung up.

After telling Darcy about her invitation, she proceeded to get ready. Rod was there in an hour's time, and she was all ready in her warm outfit of wool pants and heavy turtle neck sweater and boots. He said he was glad she had dressed warmly, and she said she was glad he didn't bring the convertible. They laughed at that, and he put his arm around her and gave her a kiss on her lips.

They did have a nice talk about what she had planned to take and the suggestions that he had for her to take. He also told her some of the things to expect to happen when they got there. He said his parents were just ordinary home people and wouldn't be expecting anything unusual from her. They knew that she was just starting out in her business and that she was working hard; also that he was crazy about her.

"Oh Rod, you didn't tell them that, did you?" Then he parked the car and turned off the engine.

He put his arm around her and pulled her closer to him and said, "I certainly did, and it's true." He placed his lips on hers, and it lasted a long time. The kiss was very warm, and she really liked it.

What is wrong with her, she thought. Is she in love with two men? That can't be it, it's not right. I can't let this go any further with him right now. His arms were around her and his cool hands started to creep up under the back of her sweater above her waist. His hands were cold but his lips were very warm on hers.

Finally she said, "Rod, we had better go now before it becomes too extreme."

He agreed and started the car and drove on.

She thanked him for the drive and all the information that he gave to her about his home life, and then he headed for her apartment and drove her home. When she arrived there, Darcy was gone, probably with Brad, she thought. Was she being envious of Darcy with having only one man to be concerned with? Would that be the way she would want it? She was thinking.

Chapter 4
The Sleigh Ride

The next week was a very busy one for Erika. She had a couple more Commissioned

Jobs to be completed plus a couple for herself that she wanted to finish before she was to leave with Rod.

Saturday was coming very fast and she had to double up on some of her work. Thank goodness for Roger; he was so great. With his help, she was able to get the most important things out and the money in.

On Tuesday she did receive a letter from her sister Rachel and Rachel agreed that it would be difficult to send something to her dad unless it was a new tractor, which he didn't know how to use anyway. Ha, ha.

As far as the boys were concerned, two of them were only interested in the women they were planning to marry soon, and the other one was thinking about a mate also. She said that they could care less.

Erika decided then that she would get them all nice, fleece-lined jackets. She knew that they could all use new ones, and she would tuck in something extra special that a girl would like, for Rachel. The next day she got all of that in the mail to them so they would have it for Christmas. She also told them not to spend any money on her as she had all she needed.

Friday night before she left the studio for home, she went over all of the things that she wanted Roger and Betsy to do before they took their holiday vacation days off. She told them she would be in touch to see how they were doing.

When she got home, she prepared all of her luggage and went over all of the new things she made or purchased for the trip to double check if they were alright. She did all of her packing so she would have everything ready when Rod picked her up in the morning.

She was so excited now. She had never made a trip with anyone before, especially a man,

Rod called her and asked if she was doing alright, and she confirmed that she was, and he said he would pick her up at her apartment about nine a.m. in the morning. She said she would be ready.

In the morning, after talking to Darcy and wishing her a good time while learning to ski at the Poconos with Brad, Darcy returned the good wishes to Erika. Rod came right on time, just before nine a.m. She was ready when he came to the door. After giving Darcy all the information as to where she could be reached and saying goodbye, Darcy wished them both lots of fun, and she and Rod were off.

It had stopped snowing for awhile, but it was still cold, and Rod turned on the heater to warm the inside of the car for her. He told her how gorgeous she looked and how she was more beautiful every time he laid eyes on her.

It was very interesting for Erika to see all the different landscapes and terrain and the different types of houses. She mentioned that to Rod and he just smiled lovingly at her.

To him, she seemed like an innocent child seeing things for the first time.

They talked about his work and exactly what he did, and then he asked her about her plans for the future in her business and just how far she planned on going with it.

She said to him, "Rod, remember I told you when I met you that my dream was to become a very prominent designer, and that is what I am still heading for. I have only been here working at this in New York for less than a year now, and I can see that I am improving in the field, and it is the career that I always wanted."

"I can see that you are determined and because of that, I think you will eventually make it. So as long as I'm around, I will always give you my support," he said.

"That is very nice of you to tell me that, Rod," she said. "It is a good feeling when you have someone at your side to support you," she told him.

A little while later Erika asked him, "How long will it take us to get there? Will it be dark when we arrive?

"It is only about one hundred and sixty or seventy miles from New York so we should definitely be there before dark. But I plan on us stopping for a little lunch around noon, and we don't need to hurry; we will make it in plenty of time, Pumpkin." There, he called her that again.

Before noon, he asked if she was hungry, and she said, "A little bit because I only had coffee for breakfast."

"Oh, then we will stop for lunch now. I could go for a little lunch now also." So he pulled off the main highway and found a nice café. It had started snowing again, and it was cold. She was glad she had brought her warm coat and scarf. She knew she would need it for sure.

After a nice hot lunch and some snuggling and embracing when they got in the car, they continued the drive. All the while it was snowing and a little difficult for Rod to see the road.

Finally, he said, "It shouldn't be too much longer darling, we are almost there."

He reached over and put his arm around her and pulled her closer to him and said, "I will try to keep you warm until we get there; just sit up close to me." Then he gave her a kiss on her forehead. Again his lips were warm against her skin.

When they had gone a little way, he said to her, "Darling why don't you relax and rest your pretty head on my shoulder and take a little nap, and I will let you know when we are getting close."

She accepted his invitation and said, "Oh that sounds good," and took him up on his offer. She snuggled her head on his shoulder and dozed off.

Finally, he nudged her and said, "Look darling, there it is, there is my old homestead; sure looks good to me."

Suddenly she sat back up in the seat and looked toward where he was pointing; it was a beautiful, very classic house with gorgeous landscaping surrounding it.

"Oh Rod, it's beautiful. I can see how it looks so good to you; it is so picturesque."

After he brought the car to a stop and parked it, he said, "Well let's get out of this thing and go in where I know it will be warm." He came around to her side of the car and ushered her to the door.

When they were inside, a man greeted him and said how glad he was to see him home again, and Rod said, "Thank you, Arnold. Would you unload the luggage from the car, please?" And then he introduced Erika to him as his very special lady friend.

Just then a very handsome couple came from the living room through the entrance to the entry, and Rod ran to them and embraced both of them. They seemed so happy to see him there.

"Mother and Dad, I want you to meet my special lady who I spoke to you about. This is Erika Beiler, and Erika, these are my parents, Bob and Alice Burton." He said this as he put his arm around her and looked deep into her eyes.

"It is so nice to meet you folks. Rod often spoke to me about you," Erika said.

"Well, Rod has certainly spoken a lot about you, when he talked to us. Every other word was 'Erika,' and it is our pleasure to finally meet you and show you our hospitality. We hope your stay here with us is very pleasant."

"I wouldn't think otherwise," Erika replied. "You are both very gracious, thank you."

"Rod, why don't you show Erika to her room, and then we will have dinner at six."

"Thank you Mrs. Burton," Erika said.

"Just call me Alice, if you like," she answered.

"Darling, let me show you your room, and then we can relax a little while before dinner." And he took her hand and led her up the winding stairway to the upper floor.

The room he showed her was magnificent. She didn't know if she could fit in with all this. It was a room for a princess, and she said that to Rod.

"My Darling, you are a princess, my princess," he said as he grabbed her in an embrace and kissed her passionately. "I am so happy you are here with me."

"Rod, you are so wonderful to me and, your parents are so wonderful. I don't know if I can live up to the expectations of all of you," she said

"Darling, just being here with me is all I expect and want." Holding her face between both of his hands, his lips met hers in a kiss that was more passionate than ever.

"Now, if you want to rest a little while and then dress for dinner, I will come up and get you before six. And the dinner is not formal," he uttered as he went out the door and closed it.

She flopped on the bed on her back and stared at the ceiling, thinking over the situation. Was she going to be accepted as Rod's special friend, or did they expect something more from this visit?

It was only for four days, so she would just wait and see.

She got up from the bed and walked around the room looking at all the lovely furnishings, and she realized then why Rod had chosen the nice furnishings in the apartment she rented from him. He was used to all things in good taste. She remembered what Ian said about him after their first date when he took her to Auriole's restaurant for dinner.

She walked over to the window and peered out and saw the snow was still falling softly, and she could see the horse stables at a distance. The view was gorgeous. There were beautiful fir trees with their branches all piled with the snow and a frozen pond in the center and a pretty gazebo next to it with evergreens planted all around it, and there were lots of Christmas decorations spotted meticulously in designated places. Everything was so picturesque. She couldn't believe that she was there.

She began to unpack her suitcase and contemplated on what to wear for dinner. She finally decided on her circular, light wool skirt in black and a very pretty silver grey V-neck sweater and a silk, black scarf wrapped around her neck with one end dangled down the back and one down the front pinned in place by a lovely brooch with silver with crystals settings.

She showered and prepared to be ready before Rod came to take her to dinner. When he came into the room, he embraced her and said, "You look absolutely gorgeous tonight, my darling Erika. How can you not win over my parents when they see you at dinner? With one look at you, they will know why I love you." She thanked him, and they went down to join his parents for dinner."

It was a lovely dinner served by a cook, and the conversations were very casual about Erika's work and how his parents liked to play golf, and Alice liked to play bridge whenever she could, and when the weather permitted, they liked to go to their summer place at Hampton on the Bay, and other things that they liked to do. They asked her what she liked to do for recreation. She said that she never had much time for anything other than her work.

Then there was small talk, and they asked questions of Erika, like how long had she been practicing designing and did she plan on continuing with that work. Erika told them that she started to have the desire to do that work ever since she was a little girl, and she had been doing it since she was in high-school and planned to pursue that as her career. They thought that was wonderful and said they admired her determination and wished her all the luck in her career.

Then they were served desserts, which were scrumptious. Erika didn't know what it was, but it was delightful. After that, the coffee was served in front of the fireplace in the living room.

Rod did most of the talking, planning on what he and Erika were going to do the next day. He suggested if Erika felt up to it that he would take her on a sleigh ride and show her the countryside.

Erika said, "That sounds wonderful. Everything looks so much like Christmas out there. I'd love to do that. Do you have a real sleigh?" she asked.

Without showing any inhibitions, he reached over and embraced and kissed her on the lips. Erika felt a little embarrassed when he did that in front of his parents. She guessed he must have known how they would accept his actions.

"That's what we shall do then," he said.

"I think that would be wonderful," his mother agreed.

"Now, I think Dad and I will leave you two love-birds and retire for the night," she said as she came over to Rod and kissed him on the cheek, and they all said goodnight.

He drew Erika closer to him and cupped her chin in his hand and looked directly into her eyes and said, "You have no idea just how happy you have made me by coming here with me, my darling Erika."

"I am very happy to be here with you also, Rod. So far it has been just out of this world for me. It has been wonderful. I'm really looking forward to the next four days here with you, I adore your parents also," she told him.

Now they were sitting side-by-side on the sofa and enjoying the fire in the fireplace. He reached over and embraced her very tightly and his lips found hers in a very passionate kiss and he said to her, "Merry Christmas, my dearest Erika. You have given me the best Christmas that I have ever had. Darling, do you know how much I love you?" he asked. "The day that I showed the apartment to you I got the strangest feeling that we were meant to be together, and I have had that feeling ever since. I have spoken to my mother about that feeling, and she seems to understand how I feel but doesn't think that I should be too pushy with you. Do you think I am too pushy?" he asked.

"No Rod, I don't think that. I know we have known each other and have been together quite a bit ever since I came here, and I know that I am very comfortable with you, and I adore you, but I believe it may take a little while longer. I told you that when you asked me the same question earlier." She looked straight into his eyes when she spoke.

120

"I realize that Erika, but I love you and want you so badly I don't know how long I can wait."

Then, he became very amorous, and his kisses became warmer as he continued kissing her. Suddenly her arms crept around his neck, and she pulled him closer as she became eager for his next kiss and his caresses as he proceeded to unbutton her sweater and his hot lips went to her neck and then down to her breast. His lips were very hot now and he was murmuring words of affection and she was enjoying it and becoming very warm inside and receptive to all of his caresses.

Realizing how much she was becoming oblivious to what they were doing, she straightened up, and buttoning her sweater said, "Rod we can't do this. Your parents will walk in and see this going on, and it will be embarrassing to both of us."

"You are right, my darling; I don't know what got into me. Yes I do. I want you so much, and I don't want to wait too long for your consent," he answered.

They agreed to call it a night and they would see each other tomorrow for that wonderful sleigh ride. He walked her quietly to her room and told her that he would meet her for breakfast in the dining room, and it would be buffet. Then with a passionate kiss, he bid her goodnight and went to his room.

It was another sleepless night for Erika as she laid there in that very spacious, luxurious bed, awake, thinking of his caresses and how much she was enamored by them. He is so loving and gentle, she thought, and I am thrilled when he kisses and caresses me. How could I not love him? She had depended on him for so much help in her life since she met him, and she felt trusting and so secure with him.

She thought about their sleigh ride tomorrow and how much fun it was going to be with him. Finally, sleep overpowered her, and she slept like a log.

The next morning, after they had a nice warm breakfast, they met Arnold in the front with the horse and sleigh and both climbed in and took off for their sleigh ride. The sleigh bells attached to the horse's reins started to jingle as they rode on, and it seemed to offer everything for a Christmas atmosphere. This was another first for her, she thought.

Rod drove all around to see the other properties all decorated festively for Christmas. It was so picturesque that it could be a Christmas card. They had a delightful time. At one point he stopped the sleigh and they got out and made snowballs to throw at each other and laughed and chased each other and tried to rub the snowballs on each other's faces. They ran and frolicked to their delight until Erika was exhausted and fell into a large snowdrift.

Rod immediately came to help her, and put his arm around her to pull her up, and his embrace brought her closer to him; then his warm lips found hers. She was thrilled and warmed throughout her body. "Oh my darling, I love you so much," he said as he caressed her face with his wet glove.

Erika thought at that time, that it was a good thing she had all those heavy snow clothes on as she might have submitted to his caresses right there.

The next couple of days were repeats of this past day—more of the snow frolicking and fun with each other. They even spent one day with him teaching her a little about skiing. She was becoming more enthralled with his touches and caresses.

At breakfast on the last day, Rod's mother announced that they would be out all day visiting some of their local friends, and they would see Rod and Erika late in the evening.

The cook would have dinner prepared for them. They were to instruct the cook to have whatever they wanted, and he was to prepare it as they desired him to do. They told Rod and Erika that they should do whatever they wanted to do and have a pleasant evening.

Rod thanked them and told them not to worry; they would be alright.

After they left, Rod asked Erika what she would like to do that day, and she said to him, "It is not snowing now, so could we just go horse- back riding?"

"That sounds like a good idea. Do you ride?" He asked.

"Oh yes, I did a lot back home but not since I've been so busy with my career. And I would love to again."

"OK, then I'll have Arnold saddle the horses up, and we'll take off," he said.

Oh, she really enjoyed that. They rode all over the hills, and it was a beautiful, sunny day, and the snow was beginning to melt in spots. They rode up a slight incline, and when they got to the top, Rod said, "Why don't we dismount, and I can show you the view below where our house is?" Erika found it was a beautiful sight.

The snow had melted on the top of this incline so Rod got the horse blanket and spread it out for them to sit on. They sat there, and he told her how his parents became owners of this property and all about his background and where he went to school and how he became interested in stocks and bonds.

Soon they were talking about their situation and how much he loved her and wanted her to be with him the rest of his life.

"Rod, I think I know how you feel, and I feel terrible to string you on this way. As I have repeatedly told you, I adore you and love being with you, but I just can't say that I am in love with you yet. I think I am, but I am not sure. If the waiting for me to make up my mind is too much for you, then I won't blame you if you decide to discontinue seeing me. I will understand," she said.

They arose from the ground, and Rod embraced her and showered her with his kisses. They mounted the horses and headed back toward his home. When they arrived there, they both said they would welcome a nice hot shower and retreated to their bedrooms and showers.

The hot shower felt so good to Erika, and after she was all finished, she threw her robe on and stepped out of the shower and into the bedroom to dress. Just as she was about to select what she wanted to wear, her bedroom door opened and Rod stood there, saying "Do you really mind if I come in?" He asked after he was already inside.

She was not prepared for this and answered. "Rod, I'm not dressed yet. I just got out of the shower."

"Yes I know. I was hoping for that. I wanted to see you when you had just gotten out of the shower and your soft, nude body was still shimmering wet," he said as he moved closer to her and embraced her.

While embracing her, he slyly unraveled her from the robe which she had wrapped around her naked body, and he let it fall to the floor.

"Rod, what are you doing? You have never behaved like this before?"

"I know darling, but my desires have overcome my sensible thinking," he said as his lips found hers in a repeatedly passionate kiss and continued downward. She felt this very hot feeling through her like she had only felt with Greg. She was all tingly inside as he kissed her all over, while the scent of her body essence lingering from the shower made him more desirous of her.

He became more amorous, and she was becoming more receptive to his caresses and discovered she wanted more. They were on the bed now and she was oblivious about what was happening but knew that she was enjoying it tremendously.

Then she realized that this was not the proper time or place. Was she sure she wanted to belong to Rod? No, she wasn't quite sure yet. Why was she so receptive to his caresses? Was she really in love with him? She didn't know what to think. So she gently pulled away from him against his struggle to tighten his embrace.

Finally, after coming back to reality, still embracing her, he said, "Darling, I am so sorry I just couldn't resist. There in my room I kept imagining you in the shower nude and stepping out with your body all shiny and wet. I was just too overcome with desire to hold you in my arms. Will you forgive me for my brashness?" he asked.

As she wrapped the robe around her naked body, she rolled over and kissed him on his brow and said to him, "Rod, how can I blame you when I think that I enjoyed accepting the caresses as much as you enjoyed the giving?"

"That makes me very happy to hear you say that. You are such an understanding person. That is one of the reasons that I love you."

When they rose from the bed, he embraced her and kissed her goodnight and told her he would see her in the morning at breakfast, and they would leave shortly thereafter. He left the room and closed the door

The next morning after they all enjoyed a nice breakfast together and Erika conveyed her thanks for an unforgettable Holiday to his folks and wished them a very merry Christmas and a happy New Year and after saying their goodbyes, she and Rod were headed for their return home.

On the drive home, she told Rod that she liked his parents very much, and she had a glorious time which she would always hold dear to her heart. They talked about all the things that they did while they were there and how much fun they had together.

He reached over and grabbed her hand and squeezed it tightly then brought it to his lips and kissed it. She looked over to him and he quickly brought his lips to her cheek.

The ride back was sort of a quiet one. They talked a lot about Erika's work, and she told him about the new fabrics that she was going to start using for her new designs.

She told him that first she planned to get one sketched up that would be magnificent, made with one of those fabrics, and she would do that just as soon as she got back to the studio. She said that she was sure that once she got that dress on one of her prominent clients, she was sure she would see her business zoom skyward.

Rod agreed with her on that. She also told him that she had decided to have her own private fashion show. He also thought that was a good idea.

Finally, the subject came to Rod's feelings about her. He said he hoped she didn't think too badly of him acting so amorous with her there in the bedroom, but he just couldn't refrain from loving her when he was so close her. He said she had to understand that his love for her was very deep and he had the feeling that she was holding back the same desires for him and wanted to help her release them.

She answered him and said, "Rod, as I told you earlier, I'm not sure yet what my feelings are for you, and I will need more time. I adore you and love being with you, but I don't know if I am ready to give my heart to you yet." Then things became quiet again for the rest of the ride home. When they arrived at her apartment he assisted with her luggage and saw her to her door and after she thanked him for the wonderful time, he thanked her for being with him for those glorious days. Then he embraced her and kissed her warmly and said he would call her later.

Chapter 5
NEW YEARS EVE

After returning home, and the trip with Rod was in the past, she really buckled down to work on her new project, and Roger and Betsy was always there to assist her in any way they possibly could.

Darcy said she had a fabulous time, and Brad taught her to ski, which made her very happy. She also said she believed that she was falling in love with Brad. He was a prince with her on the trip, and his love-making was heavenly.

Erika laughed at that, thinking of Rod's amorous love-making, and then her body became all warm when she thought of it.

Then Darcy asked Erica, "How did things go on your trip. Did you like his folks, and did you have much time alone with Rod?"

"Yes to both questions. Rod was wonderful. We had loads of fun playing in the snow. I like him more now than I ever did."

"I think that answers my questions very well," Darcy said to her.

"I wonder which one is going to be the first one to ask to spend New Year's Eve with you," Darcy said.

"I don't have any idea, but maybe I'll turn them both down if they ask and just stick to my work," was her answer.

"I have so many plans, and now I need to get busy with my work," Erika told her.

"Well you better be prepared with an answer, because I'm sure they will ask," Darcy told her.

Darcy was correct in her supposition. A few nights later, Greg called and reminded her that he had asked her to accompany him to see the condominium he was purchasing, which she had agreed to. He said he would like to go the next day if she was available. She had forgotten all about that commitment so she felt that she should agree to go. She told him that she would go but she would need to be back at the studio early afternoon. So he agreed to that.

He picked her up the next morning and took her to the new condominium that he was buying. It had an elevator to take them to the upper floors. She went in with him and looked all around at everything and thought it was very classy. Then she truthfully told him it was wonderful and very spacious. Every room had a beautiful view. She truly liked it very much and couldn't see any reason for him not to buy it.

On the way to take her to her studio, he put his arm around her and said, "Erika what are your plans for New Year's Eve?"

Oh, oh, here it comes, she thought. What am I going to say? "I haven't made any plans yet because I am so busy with my new designing procedures at the studio that I don't know if I'm going to have the time to celebrate," she told him.

"Well, I would like to celebrate the New Year with you if you can possibly find a way for that," he said as he looked yearningly at her.

She looked directly into his blue eyes and with that same tingle in her insides she said, "Greg If I can manage it, I will let you know." She started to get out of the car.

"Thank you, my sweet lady. I won't let you forget, you know," he said to her with a smile.

She smiled back at him and said, "I'm sure you won't," and departed.

It was the twenty-eighth of December when she returned to her work at the studio. She had made up her mind that she was going to be continuing designing as soon as she could. She had some requests come in for orders, and she thought she would try out the new fabrics on them to see how they would be accepted.

When she presented to the clients the designs and new fabrics, they were very receptive to her ideas. That made her very happy and gave her more confidence to go ahead with her plan. She found that she was getting very busy with orders, and the commissions were coming in.

Later she received a request from an actress who wanted something very outstanding and elegant to wear for the Golden Globe Awards. It would be high-lighted on the red carpet interviews and televised, which made it even better. Her name would be more exposed and known.

Erika accepted the commission to do it and soon she had a few more celebrities that requested something unusual and very outstanding from her. She knew she couldn't waste any time as the award ceremony would be early February, and this was the end of December. She had been commissioned to do five different gowns by this time and there were more requests coming in from other states like Virginia, California and Connecticut. She wondered how they were obtaining her name.

She mentioned this to Betsy, and Betsy replied, "Miss Erika, your name is becoming known all over the country, and you will be getting more and more requests as time goes on and they can see your beautiful designs."

Erika's reply was, "Betsy you are just too loyal to the firm that you work for, but I love to hear those compliments."

This is what she wanted to hear, and these special designs would be her advertisements. They would assist her in getting her name exposed to more prominent people and help her become a very well known designer.

Now, what she needed were a few more employees to assist her with the overload of orders coming in and more new models. She got busy and took care of that and hired some additional help immediately.

Then she needed to contact the salesman for the elegant fabrics that she wanted with her custom designs woven in the fabrics, and she also needed to increase her stock of materials. She didn't want to stock up too much on the fabrics because the orders that she was working on should be custom made and one-of-a-kind designs. She contacted him, and he assured her that he would be there the following day with some new things to show her. She was very excited about that.

The next day, he did show up with another man who he introduced as Tyler. He owned many of the factories in several places in Asia that hired local women to fabricate the elegant fabrics. He also had some very elegant samples for her to look at. Erika was very impressed with the samples and surprisingly impressed with Tyler. He was tall and well built and very handsome, sort of like the movie star, Cary Grant. His voice was low and sort of hasty, somewhat like Cary Grant. She thought when he spoke that he had a great smile with a slight cleft in his chin and very soft eyes when he looked at her.

She was attracted to him immediately and tried to direct her attention to his samples only. She didn't want to show her interest in him too much but couldn't take her eyes off him. The samples he had were obtained from a different area in Asia. They were magnificent like anything she had ever seen before. She was very impressed with them and instantly decided that they would be exactly what she was thinking about.

Tyler said it wasn't necessary for her to place a large order on each sample; she could just order what she thought she would need for each design. That would save the cost of stocking.

Erika had spent a long and fruitful afternoon with both men, and she ended up ordering much of the fabric and trims that she was going to need. When their meeting was drawing to a close her salesman, Jack, said to her, "Why don't you let us take you out to dinner? You have spent most of the day with us and did a pretty nice job of ordering, and we're sure you must be tired by now. We would like to show our appreciation, what do you say?"

Erika was tired by then and could go for a glass of wine to relax, she accepted their invitation.

They all decided to go to a little restaurant close to the studio, and the first thing they ordered was wine, since they all seemed to want wine, Tyler suggested that it would be smarter to order it by the bottle. He sat next to Erika with Jack across from them.

They were all talking about the fabrics. Erika was interested in how long it would take for her to receive her orders. Tyler assured her that he would see that she got them very soon because she had informed him of her big orders coming in. She told them a little about her trip over the Christmas holidays and that she really had a good time and enjoyed relaxing and getting her mind away from her business. Now she needed to concentrate on her business and work on her designs.

Tyler asked her if she had ever gone to Paris for their design shows. She told him that she didn't have any information about the shows there and advised him that she had not considered it since she was becoming much busier right there in New York.

Then he said, "Maybe it would be good to see what Paris had to offer. It might broaden your ideas more."

"That sounds logical. I may consider it later after I become a little more organized after losing Ian. I have had to make a drastic transition, and it has bogged me down somewhat," she informed him.

Then the subject of New Years Eve came up in their conversation, and Tyler asked her what she was going to be doing. She said, "The way my work load is looking, I haven't planned a thing. I only hope that I can take the time off to celebrate a little."

"Well, you know, it's only two days away, and Jack has to go back to Asia, but I plan on staying for the New Year's. I won't need to return until the sixth of January," Tyler told her. "I would certainly be pleased if you would join me for the occasion."

Then Jack popped up and said, "Yes, why don't you, Erika? I think that would be wonderful, and Tyler would have someone to enjoy New Year's Eve with. He needs a little fun, and who would be better to have a good time with than you?"

She thanked Jack for the compliment. Then Tyler said, "I fully agree with Jack. I think you should consider my invitation."

His remark gave her a little thrill, and she was getting the feeling that she was becoming attracted to this man, but she didn't want to show it yet.

"I'm sorry," she said. "I have an invitation for New Years, but I haven't made up my mind if I could spare the time. I sort of gave a tentative acceptance.

"If it was only a tentative acceptance, I think it would be in order to make a different decision and accept my invitation," he stated.

"Are you engaged at this time to anyone?" Tyler asked.

"No, I am not," she answered.

"Then would you agree to let me see you for New Years and also when I come back here on the sixteenth of January? I would like very much to take you out for dinner and dancing."

She had a great desire to see this man again, so after thinking a moment, she consented, saying, "Well, I could try to manage that with my schedule. I think that New Years would be alright." She wondered if she was doing the right thing, but she would like to see him on that important night.

"I will be looking forward to New Years Eve, and the sixteenth, anxiously," he said, looking at her admiringly with a loving smile.

With their dinner over, Jack served the last of the wine, and they left the restaurant.

Jack said, "Since it is getting late, may we take you home?"

She answered, "No, Jack, that is nice of you, but I can take a cab."

"No I won't hear of that. We will take you home, and then I will know where to pick you up for New Years Eve," Tyler insisted.

After resisting their offer to take her home, she finally agreed. So they took her home and bid her good night and thanked her for the big order. She thanked them for the lovely dinner. Then Tyler remembered he wanted her phone number so he could keep in touch with her for their next dates. She gave it to him, and he jotted it down on the back of her fabric order she had placed with him.

When she got into the apartment, Darcy was there nibbling on some left-over food she found in the refrigerator. She said to Erika, "Boy,

Rod has called twice looking for you, and I didn't know what to tell him. He said he tried to reach you at the studio and he got the message machine and left messages. And I was beginning to worry also.

"I'm sorry, Darcy, I should have called you. I was with these salesmen all afternoon, and when it became late, they offered to take me to dinner. By that time I was willing and hungry. My regular salesman, Jack, brought another salesman with him this time, and he carried a more extensive line of beautiful fabrics from a different part of Asia. His name is Tyler. He's good looking, and I found him very attractive—tall and well built with beautiful, slightly wavy hair streaked with a tiny bit of grey and a deep sexy voice. He reminded me of Carey Grant, the actor. He asked to take me out to dinner and dancing on the sixteenth when he comes back here. He also wants me to spend New Year's Eve with him."

"And what did you tell him, Erika?" Darcy asked

"For some strange reason, I had the urge to see him again, so I accepted the date and for the sixteenth also. I not only found him very attractive, but I got the strangest feeling that I am sort of smitten by him. When he invited me to celebrate New Year's Eve with him, I thought about Rod and Greg, so I started to decline, but my heart flipped, and I accepted the invitation. I had the desire to see him again."

"What about Rod and Greg?" Darcy asked.

"Well, Greg has asked me, but Rod hasn't, so I think I will decline both of them. What do you think?"

"To be fair about it, I think that is the best decision if they will accept your refusals without an argument," Darcy said.

"I really need to give my studio more attention and get all those great orders out," she informed Darcy, trying to make up her mind between her social engagements and her work.

She did answer Rod's calls and he asked her if she would agree to go out with him New Years Eve, and she declined saying, "Rod I have a very lengthy schedule to get out for the Grammy Awards and I really should put that time into the studio work. I don't feel that I can take the time right now," she said to him.

In a very disappointed voice he said, "But sweetheart, I haven't seen you since we returned from my folk's home, and I was looking forward to New Years with you."

"I appreciate your feelings Rod, but I do need to decline your invitation. We just spent five days together, and I have only been back to my studio a few days. You must understand, don't you?" she asked, knowing full well that he didn't. She was beginning to feel like a heel knowing how much he cared for her, and in the meantime, she had the desire to be with someone else. Why, she asked herself.

She realized that she earnestly had to get down to working on her orders now, but she was using that as an excuse to satisfy her yearning to be with Tyler.

For the next two days she worked diligently on her special orders and was pleased how they were working out. She was so happy to work on the new orders with all the new fabrics and trims, which were all delivered in time, as Tyler promised.

Before she knew it, Friday was there, the eve of the New Year, and the time for the date with Tyler. He called her that morning to remind her of their engagement. She hadn't forgotten and had her plans all together as to what she was going to wear. She was very excited and eager to see him again. It was all she could think about.

While she was dressing, the phone rang. It was Greg. "I told you that I wouldn't forget," he said.

"And I said that I was sure you wouldn't, didn't I?" was her answer.

"And what have you decided?" he asked.

"I'm sorry Greg but I made other unexpected plans for this evening so I must decline your invitation. I hope you are not too upset about that."

"Well, I am certainly disappointed. I was sure that if I waited too long for your answer it would give someone else a chance to step in, so if you have other plans, I guess I will just have to wait and try again at a later time, right?" he said.

"Oh, Greg, now you are making me feel bad, and I didn't intend it to be that way," she said to him.

"Erika, don't feel bad about it, you just go and enjoy the evening and don't worry your pretty head about me. I will have something to do. It won't be as nice as being with you, but I am sure I will enjoy the evening with my friends.

She thanked him for being so sweet in accepting her refusal and returned to finishing her dressing.

After much thought, she decided to wear her sapphire blue velvet gown, with the silver Lame' trimming that she made to wear as the host of their fashion show earlier. She also planned to style her long hair with braids across the top and a chignon in the back and wear white gold earrings with long dangles, studded with blue sapphires that matched the blue in her gown. She was satisfied that she looked very acceptable for a New Year Eve celebration.

Darcy came in and gave her approval also. She was going out with Brad to celebrate the New Year. She told Erika that she was really falling for the guy. Erika said she was happy for her and thought it was wonderful. Then she told Darcy to have a wonderful celebration with Brad.

Erika was ready when Tyler called and said he would be there in a few minutes. In a very few minutes there came a knock on the door, and there stood Tyler. Oh golly, was he so handsome in his black dress suit with the jacket trimmed in black satin and a black bow tie and satin stripes on one side of each leg of his trousers.

He spoke first and said, "You look absolutely ravishing, Erika." And with a great glow in her smile she replied, "And you, sir, look very debonair as my escort tonight."

He gave her a slight peck on the cheek and said, "You are too nice."

She didn't know where he was taking her, but she thought it must be very nice or he wouldn't be dressed like he was.

As he started to drive off, he handed her a bouquet—an orchid wristband corsage.

"Oh, Tyler, it's beautiful. I've never had an orchid in my entire life," she said as she placed it on the wrist of her left hand. She didn't know if that was the correct hand or not. Then she reached up and kissed his cheek.

They drove on, and he put his arm around her shoulders and said, "I have chosen a place to go for dinner and dancing, and I hope you approve of it."

"I trust your taste so I am sure it will be fine. I probably wouldn't know the difference anyway since I haven't had a lot of night-life since I've been here," she assured him.

"Well it is the 21 Club. It is very famous, and it is about a hundred years old. A lot of famous celebrities frequent the restaurant, and the food is excellent," he told her. "I have never been there for New Years Eve, but I thought it would be interesting for the both of us. I did have quite a difficult time getting the reservations. If I had been a little bit later I would have been out of luck."

"That's sweet of you, Tyler, but wherever we went would have been fine with me. It is very nice of you to do this."

"I really did want to spend this evening with you, Erika, and I wanted it to be a very special night for both of us." He looked at her and squeezed her hand. She could feel his eyes on her while he was driving so she looked up at him and he looked at her and pursed his lips in a motion of a kiss and gave a squeeze of her shoulders.

Why did that give her thrill? She could feel the tingle go through her body. Is he too handsome to be a good man? Why did he attract her differently from Rod or Greg? They are both very good looking and very sweet to her. Well, she decided, she was going to enjoy being with him and have a good time this evening with this new escort. This was the first time she had ever been out to celebrate a New Years Eve with a man.

When they arrived at the club, the valet took the car, and they entered through a fancy gated entrance with statues of a Jockey on each side of the entrance and many statues repeated all around the top of the lobby area.

She said to Tyler, "The person who owns this place must be a race horse jockey. Is he Tyler?"

"No, sweetheart, he just caters to that crowd." And he squeezed her hand.

When they got inside they were greeted by a Maitre d'. Erika was absolutely amazed at what she saw. She could see in the Bar Room; the huge ceiling was covered with toys and all kinds of memorabilia. All of those items were very interesting to her. Then the Maitre d' ushered them to the upstairs dining room where everything was very elegant, including famous paintings on all the walls.

They were seated at a secluded table in the corner, and it seemed very private. She was informed later that the upstairs dining room was only for very important people. All around it seemed as though the entire place was filled with important people. Erika felt very important being there in the company of Tyler.

Tyler ordered for both of them with cocktails first. After having many cocktails, during which time Tyler was very endearing, caressing and kissing her. She was very receptive to his feelings. After being on cloud nine from his caresses, they were served the dinner. The cocktails were very warming to Erika, and she found the dinner to be absolutely superb.

They talked about both of their lives—some things about her past life and where she came from and things about her career. He told her that he was originally from Wyoming and moved to California when he was nineteen years old—he was twenty-six years old now. He started out being an importer of things from the orient and finally took on the importing of fine fabrics. One thing led to another, and now he was the owner of fabric factories in Asia. He had a home in Santa Barbara, California, and that was his base. He said he had to go to Asia about every three months, but he loved living in California. As he gave her an endearing smile, he said, "I hope that someday soon you will come to love California also."

Then Erika said to him, "I understood that you were a salesman, the same as Jack, but had a different territory. What is the difference?" she asked.

"Well, the only difference is that I own some of the Asian factories and Jack does not. You might say that I employ salesmen, but we both sell merchandise. Jack and I have known each other for three or four years now, and we have become good friends."

After their dinner, which lasted a long time she thought, they were ushered downstairs for dancing and given all kinds of noise makers in preparation for the celebration when the New Year arrived. They danced with the lights low, and Tyler held her very close. He was taller than her, but he cradled her head to his neck and put both of his arms around her body and pressed her body close to his. She could almost feel his heart beat. Between dance numbers, he raised her head and kissed her on the lips. They were very soft, warm kisses.

Then he said to her, "Erika, this has been the most beautiful evening I think I have ever experienced, and you have been the loveliest cause of that. I really want to see you again if you will permit me. Do you think that you could?"

Before she could answer him, the bells and horns of all of the noise-makers went off, and everyone was yelling. He couldn't hear what she was saying. She looked around and everyone was kissing each other. Suddenly he embraced her and lifted her up and spun her around, gleefully, and kissed her passionately with his soft lips to hers. The thrill went clear down to her toes. She was sorry when it was all over because she wanted more.

After everything settled down, he said to her, "Erika, you didn't answer the question that I asked before the ruckus."

"I'm sorry, what was the question again?' she asked.

"I really want to see you again, if you will permit. Do you think that you could?" he asked, repeating his question to her.

"Tyler, this has been a wonderful experience, celebrating a New Years Eve with you tonight, so I can't think of a single reason why I wouldn't want to see you again. You are a very nice gentleman."

"That's good enough for me, so you better expect to hear from me soon," he said with a broad smile.

It was about three o'clock in the morning by the time he took Erika home. He snuggled her close during the entire drive. He delivered her to her door, and they embrace each other, and he kissed her passionately with those wonderful soft lips and said, "Erika, I don't want to let you go, but I guess I must. I will call you in a couple of days and let you know when I will be back in New York. I think it will be very soon, and I will expect to see you again if you permit. They kissed again, and he said with a grin, "Goodnight or is it good morning?"And she laughed and went inside and closed the door.

She leaned against the closed door and felt the thrill go through her body, thinking of him. She couldn't believe how wonderful he was and what a great evening she had experienced with him and what he did to her feelings. She seemed to be thrilled with his every touch He was so affectionate and caring. She loved the way he held her while they danced. It had been so long since she had danced with a man.

After she went to bed, she couldn't go right to sleep even though she was tired from the big night. She kept thinking about Tyler and Rod and Greg. The feeling that she had for Tyler was very different from the feelings she had for either Greg or Rod. She did like both of them very much, but it seemed that they had only awakened her sexual feelings which had never been aroused before. With Tyler it seemed as though he didn't come on strong, and she found she wanted that maybe more than he did. She decided that when she was with him she really wanted him. What was there about him that drew her like a magnet? Was he the one she really loved and wanted? Would he call her again? Or would this just be a passing acquaintance for him? How would she handle Rod and Greg? She still seemed to have deep feelings for Rod and Greg, but had they just awakened her inner desires, which she never had a chance to experience before?

Thinking of all different ways she would tell them, she finally dozed off to sleep. It was after noon when she was awakened by the phone.

When she answered it, Tyler said, "Good afternoon, sleepy head, how do you feel today?"

A thrill went through her body just hearing his voice. "Gee I don't know yet; my eyes are barely open. It looks like a beautiful day though," she said to him.

"I talked to my base in California, and it's not important for me to go back there until the tenth of January. S-o-o-o when can I see you again?" he asked.

"Well, let me think, I do need to get back to the studio Monday and start on the Golden Globe orders and give instructions to my new help. I have so many requests on my desk that I need to get straightened out," she said, thinking out loud.

"Listen, sweetheart, I don't want to make it difficult for your business, but don't you think you could work some time out for me to be with you for at least one night? I would really like to see you again before I leave, perhaps Wednesday—that would be the fifth and that would give you a couple of days to make adjustments at work. I will be leaving here the following week, on Monday."

While she hesitated, he said, "It will be a long time until Wednesday, but I do look forward to being with you again," he said.

She felt a thrill when he said he wanted to be with her again and replied, "I suppose that I could work it out to be with you Wednesday." He seemed very happy that she was accepting his invitation.

The next few days were very busy getting all of her commissioned requests in order and setting the new help up with what she wanted them to do. Roger was a great help seeing that they were doing everything the correct way, according to what Erika wanted.

Things were going along very smoothly and her schedule was right on time—for finishing the orders that she had, and the designs were exquisite. She was very happy with them. All her help raved about them and she was anxious to have the clients see them. When she presented the finished products to them, they were delighted.

She couldn't wait until Wednesday was there. In the meantime, she had a call from Rod, and he wanted to see her the next night. She explained to him that she would not be available.

He said to her, "Darling, why are you putting me off like this, did I do something wrong? You must know how I feel about you and that I yearn to see you?"

"Rod, you didn't do anything wrong, and I don't feel that I am putting you off. I do like you and like being with you. I feel that you are a very close friend, but I have never made any definite commitments to you. I would see you if I was available, but I am not right at this time," she responded.

"Well, do you think that sometime when I call you that you might find time to see me?"

"Certainly Rod, you will always be my dear friend," she assured him.

After asking her how her business was going and her telling him about all the new fabrics that she was going to be using, they bid each other to have a good day and hung up.

The next day, when she and Darcy were talking about their latest events, Darcy asked her how her New Years Eve date was, and Erika told her all about Tyler and how she felt about him. Darcy said she thought she passed over Rod alright, but what was she going to do about Greg? She told Darcy that she had a very definite opinion about Greg's feelings and didn't know just how she would handle that. Darcy asked her if she thought that she would still have that feeling if she looked into Greg's blue eyes now—what was she going to do about that.

Erika answered her, saying, "I am just going to see how I feel about Tyler after I see him a few times, and if he thrills me like I think he will that should let me know that he is meant for me."

"Well then, let me know how you come out with this problem," Darcy said to her with a grin on her face.

"By the way how was your New Years Eve with Brad," Erika asked.

"Oh golly, it was wonderful. We went out dancing, and he proposed to me. He wants us to have a June wedding. I was shocked but thrilled.

I didn't give him a definite answer yet. Do you think I should get to know him better? I do love him, but I don't know if he loves me as much," she said to Erika.

"June is a few months away so maybe you will know him better by then. Tell him to ask you again a couple of months from now. What do you think?" she asked, looking at Darcy questioningly. "I think you're right," she answered.

Erika was so anxious for Wednesday to get there, and she couldn't make up her mind as to what she was going to wear. She surmised that he would take her someplace very nice so she picked out what she thought was the best.

Since the weather was still cold, she chose a lavender colored flared skirt and a violet angora sweater with a white leather three-quarter-length coat and white boots and white scarf with fringe. Then she wondered if she would be able to keep her mind on her work until Wednesday got there.

Finally, it was Wednesday, and she left the studio early and hurried home. As she entered, the phone was ringing, and she picked it up, and it was Tyler. "Hi Erika, I wasn't sure if you would be home yet or not. I just took a chance to call you and see if we were still on for tonight," he asked.

"Don't you remember that I told you tonight would be alright, and Tyler, I don't forget my appointments, especially those that are important to me. I just got in from the studio a few minutes ago, and I'm looking forward to seeing you," she informed him.

"Darling, I remember, but I just wanted to make sure you didn't have something else come up. What time would you like me to pick you up?" he asked.

"I will need about an hour to shower and dress, so in an hour would be fine." "That's fine, I can hardly wait. I'll see you in an hour," he assured her

In an hour he was there knocking on her door. She was ready, and she opened it and greeted him and asked him to come in. He did and asked her if there was anyone else there and she said, "No, why?" He grabbed her and embraced her tightly and put his soft lips on hers then said, "I just wanted to hold you and kiss you but I didn't want to intrude on your roommate if she was here."

"No she is not home yet. She should be coming any minute if she comes right home after work. I never know. We go our own way and do our own things; we find it better that way."

"You are wonderful, plus beautiful," he said as he kissed her again.

They left and drove to the restaurant that Tyler had picked out, which was Auriole's.

"Oh this is a wonderful restaurant. I was here before with someone else." She informed him.

When she said that, he turned to her and said, "If that is the case, I want to take you some place different." So they turned around and he found another restaurant that he said was very cozy and the food good.

She didn't remember the name of it, but it looked very romantic inside, and they were seated in a very private booth. He snuggled up close to her and put his arm around her and kissed her as they waited for the waiter to approach then. He asked her what she would like to drink. She said that she would take whatever he ordered as long as it wasn't something to knock her out.

He looked at her in a questioning way and said, "Erika, What do you think of me. Do you think that I would do that to you?"

"I'm sorry. I just meant that I hoped it wasn't too strong," she said. So he ordered a bottle of champagne, and the waiter poured him a taste first, and he approved. Then he poured Erika's. The drink was very warm going down, and she was enjoying it.

Tyler asked her if she would like him to order, and she agreed. After the order was placed, he said to her, "You made me very happy that you accepted my invitation to take you out again tonight. Do you know what I think? I think I'm falling in love with you. I want to feel you close to me," he said, looking directly into her eyes.

She was so thrilled by his statement that she had the desire for him to grab her and take her to heaven. Instead she said to him, "Are you real sure, Tyler?" Then he embraced her again and found her lips for another soft kiss. This time his lips were hot and he didn't want to let her go from his embrace.

Suddenly he released his embrace as the waiter was there to serve their dinner and bring another bottle of champagne. She was beginning feel all warm inside as the sips went down. She didn't remember what the dinner was like but she ate most of it. All the while he was caressing her arms and back and kissing her.

When the dinner was finished, he said to her, "Would you like to go someplace where we could have a little more privacy, and I could feel better about holding you close to me?" "Would you agree to that?"

"So where would we go for that?" she asked.

"We could go to my hotel if that would be alright with you. I wouldn't want you to go if you objected."

"Tyler, you know it isn't proper for a lady to accompany her escort to his room. I don't think it would look good, do you?" she asked.

"Darling, you are absolutely correct in your thinking, but I want to hold you so very close, and I can't do that here. Can you understand?" he asked.

Then she asked herself, was she feeling the same and wanting the same thing. She wanted more from him, but she didn't want to spoil what they had going so she said, "Tyler, I don't think that would be appropriate at this time. Maybe after we got to know each other a little better I wouldn't feel this way." She wanted so much to be with him longer but didn't want him to think that she was easy.

He seemed a little disappointed but said he agreed with her. Then he suggested that they take a drive and he would stop someplace where he could embrace her and kiss her where nobody would notice. She agreed to that. He drove along the bay and parked, and they talked about all sorts of happenings.

She told him about Jody and how she and Darcy felt very bad for both Jody and Dan; bad for Jody for what she went through and very sad for the way it affected Dan. She also told him about her boss, Ian, being murdered and how she really missed his support and the story about why his lover killed him. Now she had to pick things up and move on without Ian's guidance with her design work.

He put his arms around her and said, "You know what, Erika, you will do just fantastic. You have the talent and the fortitude to go ahead and I for one, have lots of faith in your ability." When he said that, she raised her head up and gave him a very sweet kiss on his soft lips and he accepted that with a strong embrace.

When they were all talked out, he said to her, "Darling, I have to see you again before I leave, could we arrange that?"

"When do you want us to see each other again?" She asked, hoping he would say tomorrow because she was anxious to see him again but she didn't want him to know that.

He thought awhile and then said "Could we get together on this Friday, would that be alright with you?"

"Friday" She exclaimed, realizing that it was just a day away. "That is the day after tomorrow."

"Would that be too far away for you? It is for me, but if that is the earliest we can make it, I think I could bear to wait that long," he said.

She laughed at his remark and said, "Friday will be OK with me."

"Friday it is then. I will call you tomorrow and confirm that."

They hugged and kissed a little while longer, and then he drove her home and said, "Goodnight my love. I'll call you tomorrow and confirm our date for Friday," and he went down the stairs, heading for his car.

Tomorrow was another wintry day with the snow coming down, but Erika didn't mind it as she kept thinking about Tyler. She went to the studio and worked diligently on her orders. Everything was coming out to her expectations on her designs, which made her happy.

Around the middle of the day, she received the call from Tyler, and he said, "Hi my sweet Erika, how are you on this snowy and wintery day?"

"Oh I am fine. Is it too cold for you here in the snow? he asked. "I would think that you would be accustomed to the California warm weather since you are acclimatized to that."

"Well I have been here several times when it was snowing so I don't mind it," he answered. "How is your day going at the studio?"

"Oh, everything is coming along great," she told him.

"I told you that I would call you to confirm our date tomorrow, so is it still on?"

"Yes, Tyler it is still on," she assured him.

"Well then, I will see you at about seven at your place, is that OK? I can feel your closeness already, and I can hardly wait," he said. She didn't want to let him have any idea that she felt the same way and that she was getting all jittery already with just the thought of being with him. So in a very cool tone she said to him, "Yes, Tyler that will be fine."

Then he said, "I'll see you at seven tomorrow then. Bye love." and they ended the call.

On her way home from the studio, she was thinking about what she was going to wear tomorrow for her date with Tyler. He would probably just take her out to a restaurant for dinner, but she didn't have any idea what his plans would be for the rest of the evening. She would wait and see.

Tomorrow was another work day that seemed to go very slow for her thinking about her date with Tyler that night. The picture of his face loomed in front of her all day, and it was hard for her to concentrate on her work.

When she got home, Darcy was there and they talked a little about each one's day. Darcy said that she was becoming madly in love with Brad and thinking more about their marriage than ever. She said "I think about him all day long and can't wait to see him after I get off work. He is so sweet to me and so affectionate. I never thought that he would be the man that I would fall madly in love with."

Then Erika said to Darcy, "I guess we are both madly in love."

"Why, do you say that? Have you decided that you are really in love with Tyler?" Darcy asked her.

"I am in a quandary yet because I get all jittery when I think of him, and he hasn't made any drastic passes at me as yet, but he says he wants to be near me. Maybe I will get more of a feeling as to whether he wants me or not when I see him tonight. If I get a strong feeling for him and I decide I am in love with him, then what will I do when he goes away?" she asked, looking at Darcy sadly.

"Maybe he will give you some strong indications tonight when you are with him. Then you will need to decide if you are in love with Rod or not. Remember, I told you Rod was mad about you," Darcy replied. Erika didn't know what to say about that.

When Erika entered her bedroom to dress for her date with Tyler she thought about what she should wear. Since it was snowing, she chose the warm beige pants that she made for her snow trip with Rod and a red turtleneck zippered sweater with her beige boots and the beige coat with the fur trim.

That made her think of Rod and how much he wanted her. Why didn't she want him that much? But she couldn't think of that now as she had to look good for Tyler.

She decided she would wear her hair in braids. So she proceeded to get ready. The more she thought about Tyler, the more excited she got. After she had her shower, she became calmer and seemed to feel better.

It was nearing seven o'clock and soon Tyler would be knocking on her door. The phone rang and Darcy answered it. "It's for you, and I think it is Greg." she said while handing it to Erika.

"Hi, Greg," Erika greeted him. "How are you?"

"I just called to see how you were doing and if you had any time to go out with me. It has been quite a while since we have seen each other, and I miss you," he said to her.

"Yes Greg, it has been awhile, but I have been pretty busy at the studio. I have an engagement tonight, but why don't you call me in a few days and I will see how my schedule at the studio is?"

"Erika, you know I am getting the feeling that you are trying to brush me off. If that is true, please tell me, and if you just want to be friends, then make that clear to me."

"Greg, I did try to make that clear to you previously. I said that I couldn't make a commitment to you, but I would still like to be a friend to you? Do you remember?" she asked him.

"Yes Erika I do remember, and you are right, but that doesn't change the fact that I love you and want to be with you."

"Greg, I can see you as a friend, but someone else came into my life, and I feel that I should tell you that. You have been a dear friend, and I will always feel that way about you. Can you understand that?"

"Yes Erika, I can understand now how you feel, and I thank you for bringing me up to date. I know where I stand and will always think about you as a sweet, dear friend, and if you ever need a real friend, please remember me, and I will be there."

"Thank you, Greg," she said, and they closed their conversation.

Erika felt good about her talk with Greg because now she wouldn't feel bad about how she had held him off.

In a very few minutes there was a knock on the door, and Erika surmised that it would be Tyler, so she answered, and there he stood as good looking as ever. He was just as she had imagined him while she was working all day at the studio.

"Hi my Erika," he greeted her. "You look as lovely as always, I'm glad that you are wearing something warm as it is cold outside."

Just then, Darcy appeared from her room, and Erika introduced the two of them.

"Don't be worried if Erika is not home early as I am going to hang on to her for a very long time tonight. I want to remember this night while I am gone away from her," Tyler said to Darcy as they were departing.

Darcy laughed and said to him, "I won't worry because I know she will be in good hands." Then she said "Goodnight and have a good time." And they went out the door with Tyler's arm around Erika.

As soon as they reached his car and he turned the heater on to warm her, he cupped her face with his hands and kissed her passionately on her lips. Then he asked her where she would like to go for dinner. She told him to make the choice as she wasn't sure which restaurants would serve good food. He said he knew of a place that he thought she would like. So they decided that was where they would go.

When they got into the restaurant and the maitre d' showed them a table that was sort of secluded, Tyler said, "That's just fine." And he told the waiter to bring champagne as this was sort of a going away dinner.

As they were both served the wine, Tyler said he wanted to give a toast to Erika and he raised his glass to Erika and said, "This is to my lovely lady, and I hope and pray that she will be here for me when I return, which will be too long for me to be away from her."

Then he brought his glass up, and they clicked their glasses together. She smiled at him lovingly and said "The lady will be here waiting when the man returns, if that is what the man would like." Then he reached over and kissed her.

They had several glasses of the wine, and Erika was warming up fast. Finally, Tyler asked her what she would like to order, and she said she was leaving it up to him. So he ordered for both of them and poured more wine.

During their meal, they talked about Tyler going away, and he asked her if she had ever thought of going to California.

"You mean for a visit or permanently? She asked.

"Well, now that you ask, I mean permanently, with me," he answered.

"But Tyler, what would I do about my business? She asked. "I've worked and planned so long for what I've got now

"I know you have, darling. We'll talk about that later. Right now I want to take you in my arms and love you. If there was just somewhere we could go where I could love you like I want to," he said. She knew in her heart that she wanted this man as much as he wanted her. All during their dinner she imagined how it would be to have him make passionate love to her.

"Do you think you could agree to go to my hotel this last night that we are together, before I leave?" he asked in a pleading sort of way. By this time the champagne was working on her resistance, and finally, reluctantly, she agreed, knowing that she also wanted him to hold her close.

They were finished with their dinner, which neither of them consumed entirely, but they finished the champagne, which Erika found very invigorating and warming to her love buds. Then they decided to leave with both of them seemingly on cloud nine. It wasn't very far to his hotel, and after parking the car, he ushered her up to his suite.

After taking her coat and offering her a chair, he said to her, "This isn't what you deserve darling, for me to entertain you, but this is what I have at the moment so it will have to do for now, and at least we can be alone. Do you mind darling?"

"I'm not here to give my opinion on your room, Tyler. I'm here to be with you." It seemed as though he couldn't wait to embrace and kiss her passionately.

They talked a little while about his place in California and how long he had been there and why he liked it there. She understood how he liked it there so well. Then they got on the subject of her moving out there.

"You would love it there, my darling," he said. "The weather there is usually always nice and sunny."

"Tyler, don't you understand how I feel about my business? I can't just drop it and leave it," she pleaded.

"Erika, I don't mean for you to leave your designing business. You could have a studio out there, and we could be together. I am asking you to marry me so that we can be together forever," he said to her.

"But Tyler, you have never proposed to me. We have not known each other very long, so are you sure you want to marry me?" she asked.

"Yes, I am sure that you are the woman I want, but how do you feel?" he asked.

"Gosh Tyler, this is so sudden for me that I think I will need a little time to think about it. There is so much to consider about a change like that," she answered.

Then he said to her, "Erika, I am proposing marriage to you, and if you need time to think about it, you can do that while I am gone, and then I will expect your acceptance when I come back, and I won't take no for an answer." Then he embraced her and kissed her again.

Finally, he suggested they find a more comfortable place for both of them to sit together. He took her by her hand and invited her to sit next to him on the sofa. His kisses were becoming more warming to Erika, and his caresses were thrilling her like she had never been thrilled before. She was beginning to be quite receptive and seeming to return his feelings. She had a strong desire for this man. His kisses became warmer and warmer, and she was becoming more desirous of him and didn't want him to stop. She had no experience of someone loving her like this before. She had never encountered anyone that she desired as much as she desired Tyler. What was this desire she had? She asked herself.

While he was talking, he was kissing her eyes, then her nose, then her neck, and his lips were very soft and warm on her skin. She was oblivious of him removing her sweater and finally finding her firm breasts. She was all excited inside now, and in between his kisses she whispered to him, "Tyler this can't be right. We have only known each other a very short time, and I don't really know you." As he kissed her ear, he whispered, "Darling, I have no doubts about wanting you because I have looked the world over to find the one I love, and I have found her, and I don't ever want to lose her.

"Then he said to her, "Darling, whatever we do together is right because I have fallen madly in love with you so much that I feel I want you with me forever," he said to her as he continued to bring his lip to hers. "But one thing is for sure. If you are not feeling the same as I, or you feel that this is repulsive to you, I will stop loving you and not impose on you any longer. Do I make that very clear to you?"

Oh yes, she understood that he was definitely in love with her, but was she truly in love with him she asked herself. Definitely, she was enjoying every bit of his love and caresses. Tyler was stroking her beautiful, long blonde hair and kissing her eyes and neck, and they talked about feelings for each other and what was in the future for them.

He said he didn't want to go back to California without her. He wanted her to be with him forever. She told him that she would earnestly consider what she could do. Maybe she could open a branch studio and travel back and forth if that could be worked out. All the while he was caressing her. Then Erika decided she would take a shower and prepare for leaving to go home

After she had completed her shower, he came out of the room and into the bathroom to see her step out of the shower. Looking at her lovely, nude body, he said to her, "My darling, I just can't take my eyes away from your body. How can I leave you and go to California without you? You are driving me crazy. I don't want to leave you," he said, embracing her and caressing her smooth body.

Hearing him say that reminded her of when Rod looked at her nude when she stepped out of her shower at his parent's place. For some reason she couldn't explain, it thrilled her thinking of Rod and that night in the bedroom at his parents' home.

After they dressed, they decided it was time to take Erika home, but before he left her, he said he wanted one more night with her before he went. She asked him, "What night would that be Tyler?"

"How would Sunday night work out for you? Could I see you Sunday night because my flight is Monday and that will give me a lot of you to dream about during my flight? I will think about you stepping out of the shower shimmering wet. That will make me want to get right back to you." They agreed on that and prepared to leave his suite.

When they got to Erika's apartment, Erika asked him in for a minute and went to see if Darcy was home yet. Darcy wasn't home so Erika felt it safe for them to embrace and kiss goodnight.

Then Tyler said to her, "I'm asking you again Erika, I want to marry you. I want you with me forever. Will you promise me that?" he pleaded. "I need you and I expect your answer by the time I come back." They stood near the door of her apartment and embraced.

Then for the fourth or fifth time, Erika repeated to him, "Tyler, do you realize that we have not known each other very long and have only been together just a few times, which have been unforgettable, but how can we be sure that we are meant for each other? This may only be a passionate fantasy?"

He said to her, "You and I will both know while I am gone. I know I will be longing for you and waiting for the time to be back with you, and if you yearn to have me near you, then we will know for sure, right? I will see you Sunday night. And I'll call you tomorrow."

Saddened by the thought of their parting and his leaving for California, they kissed and reluctantly pulled away from each other as he said, "Goodnight my love" and went out the door.

Needless to say, she didn't sleep a wink for hours. She just could not seem to get Tyler off of her mind. She kept feeling his kisses and caresses that he had given her earlier and she did not want to let go of it. How was she going to get through the days when he was gone to California? Was she going to be able to work without missing him and yearning for him? How soon would he be back to her? Does he love her enough to come back to her? He said he did, but could she believe him? There was a feeling of fear inside of her that he might not come back. What would she do if he did not come back? Thinking of all of those things seemed to just wear her out, and sleep finally found her.

The next morning was Thursday and a work day for Erika. She had to go to the studio today and get busy on her special orders. It was difficult as her thoughts kept going back to Tyler. He was leaving Monday she remembered. Would he call her before he left? She desperately wanted to hear his voice again before he left her. She had to get her mind clear and concentrate on her work. She was trying to wrap up the work she had to do for the Golden Globe Awards. A lot of the requests came from California, and they would require being fitted on models having the exact sizes of the actresses who would be wearing them, so it was a lot of work for Erika, and there could not be any errors.

Her spirits were pleasantly lifted when in the middle of the afternoon she received a call from Tyler. She was really happy to hear his voice. "Are you very busy?" he asked. "Not real busy," she answered.

"I just wanted to hear your voice, but I don't mean to interfere with your work," he told her.

"It's alright. I have a few minutes," she replied.

"I was just thinking of you and our date for Sunday and could feel you in my arms already. Do you think you will be able to arrange that?" He asked.

"Yes, that would be fine. I won't need to go to the studio on that day," she said, confirming his request.

"Is seven o'clock alright with you?" he asked.

"Oh yes, that's fine," was her answer.

"I'll see you on Sunday at seven then." he said to her.

"OK," she answered, hanging on to hear his voice a little longer on the phone; she didn't want him to go, but finally she hung up.

Could it just be her or was the time going too slow until Sunday when she would see Tyler again? It seemed to drag along for her. She was so thrilled that he called her and wanted to see her again before he left.

On Saturday she received another call from Tyler, and he sounded very distraught and saddened. He told her that an emergency came up that made it very necessary for him to leave immediately for California, and he would not be able to keep their date for Sunday. "I was really looking forward to seeing you one more time before I departed. I thought then I could keep the image of you close to my heart until I would see you again," he said

"What happened, Tyler?" she asked "Are you alright?"

"I love you, my darling, remember that, and I'll tell you all about it when I get back, but I must go now to make my flight. You take care of my property until I return; you know what I mean. See you soon and remember that I really love you." And he was gone.

You could have knocked her over with a feather from that call. She was so stunned she didn't know what to think. It was so sudden and unexpected. What was happening to Tyler? Now she had a very strong feeling that she had fallen in love with him. She didn't want anything to happen to him. She wanted him to come back to her.

He didn't say he would call her later or anything like that. So what could it be to take him away so suddenly?

Chapter 6
A DISAPPOINTMENT

The week-end passed and not a word from Tyler. Could she bear this? She felt very sure that he was sincere about his feelings for her, but why didn't he call her? She was very sad all weekend. Monday came around, and Erika made up her mind to load herself down with her work, and that way she would have a better chance not to have Tyler on her mind constantly. She was receiving inquiries and orders from all parts of the world now. She was working hard and staying very busy to keep from thinking about Tyler. Maybe he didn't really love her like he said he did. Why would he lead her on like he did? He seemed so sincere. She just had to quit thinking of these things so she could work.

One week passed and still no word from Tyler. What could possibly be a reason for him not to call her after being gone a week, she thought. Surely he would call if he loved me as he said.

After two weeks passed and no word, she was very distraught. She was beginning to think he had really deserted her for good. Then she decided that she would question her other salesman Jack when he came in to take her orders for fabrics. Maybe he would know something about Tyler since they were friends. ¹She would need to wait until he came in, and she didn't know exactly when that would be. She was bearing down on her work to keep her mind clear of Tyler, but it wasn't easy. Even Roger and Betsy noticed that something was bothering her severely.

A week or two later at the studio, she received a call from Greg. "Hi Erika, how are you doing? I haven't heard from you for some time. Am I on your low list?" he asked.

"Oh no, Greg, why are you saying that?"

"Well, it seems that you are shying away from me. Did I do something wrong?" he said.

"No Greg, you haven't done anything wrong. It's just that I have been so very busy here at the studio that I haven't had much time."

"Do you think that you could spare some time to have dinner with me at my new apartment soon? I would like you to be with me for the christening of it with a dinner together, just you and I. What do you say?"

She mulled it over in her mind and thought maybe that would be what she needed to get Tyler off of her mind a little. She couldn't go on like this forever. Maybe he was never coming back.

"That's very nice of you, Greg. What night would that be?" she asked.

"Let's see, this is Wednesday, so how about Friday evening? Could you make that? I can pick you up around seven, would that be a good time for you?"

"Yes, Greg that will be fine," she agreed.

"Then it's a date, and I'll see you Friday," he said and hung up.

Erika hadn't seen Greg for several weeks so she wondered how he would act toward her. Would he be amorous or just a gentleman and how were her feelings toward him going to be? She questioned herself. Were his eyes still going to set her off drowning into them again? She would just have to see. She felt it would be nice to get out with someone else and maybe have Tyler out of her mind for a little while. Could anyone else possibly put Tyler out of her mind, she asked herself.

Friday, a little before seven, Greg was there to pick her up. When she answered the door, she saw that he was dressed very nice and looked good to her. He put his arm around her and kissed her on the cheek. She noticed that his lips were warm as usual. When they arrived at his new apartment, he ushered her in and she noticed that everything was set up for a very elegant dinner. Then she asked him "Did you do all of this Greg? Everything is set up so beautifully."

"No, as a matter of fact I hired a maid to cook and set it all up the way I wanted it to be. This is a very special occasion for two reasons, one to christen my new home, and the other to have you here with me." He embraced her and kissed her on her lips with his very warm lips. Then he guided her to the sofa and said as he placed the wine and glasses on the cocktail table "If it's agreeable with you, we will have our wine here first and then I will serve dinner."

"That's wonderful, Greg, but can't I help you?"

"No, I want you to just sit there and let me serve you," he said as he poured the wine.

After pouring her wine, he picked up his glass and came over and sat close to Erika on the sofa. After they talked about her business and how it was going, she asked him if he had any help in decorating his apartment. He told her that he hired an interior decorator to help him. "Well she certainly has done a great job," she informed him. He thanked her and found her lips again for another warm kiss. When he leaned over to kiss her, she looked directly into his eyes but all she saw was the pretty color and got no special feelings from them at all. She knew then that her passion for Greg was gone, but she still wanted to remain friends with him because he was such a sweet guy.

She asked him, "Do you have a special person that you care for that you are seeing now?"

"I was hoping it would be you, but it seems that you must have given your heart to someone else," he said to her, looking directly into her eyes.

She kissed him on the cheek and said, "Why don't we have dinner first and then I will tell you about me?"

The dinner was delicious but it seemed that it was difficult for both of them to really enjoy it. It consisted of veal cordon bleu with scalloped potatoes and endive salad.

When they had enough to eat, they just sat and talked. Greg told her he had been very busy selling a lot of commercial buildings and had invested in a few of them as well. He had been seeing a young woman he knew from another real estate firm, and although she could never fill the place in his heart that Erika did, he was beginning to like her and enjoyed being with her.

Erika said to him, "I'm so happy for you, Greg, and I hope she appreciates how wonderful and dear you are, and I hope she makes you very happy because you deserve it."

"Thank you, dear Erika. Now tell me what has happened to you? I know you don't feel the same about me, so there must be someone else, right?"

"Yes, Greg, there is someone else, and I think that I may be falling in love with him. The only problem is that he went away, and I haven't heard from him, and it is breaking my heart not knowing that he is alright."

Before she realized it, she was telling him all about Tyler and how he promised to be in touch with her and that he wanted to marry her.

Greg tried to console her by saying, "I know you will hear from him. There must be some very important reason that he is not contacting you. From what you have told me, I am sure that he loves you. And from my own experience of being with you, he would definitely be in love with you."

"You have made my heart a little lighter, Greg, and I want you to know that you will always have a small part of my heart, and I will always remember what a dear person you are." And she planted a kiss on his brow, and he embraced her fondly.

When she told Greg about Tyler, her thoughts immediately went to Rod. Why hadn't she told him about her feelings for Tyler, she wondered? Well, if he came back to her, and she found that she was really in love with him, it would be important to tell him.

She thanked Greg for the lovely evening with an excellent dinner and the advice he had given her. Then she asked him if he would mind taking her home, which he politely agreed to do.

She was so upset from not hearing from Tyler that she kept thinking about what she should do.

When she arrived home, she was thinking about the whole situation and about what Tyler had said to her about going to Paris to obtain more ideas for her designs. After mulling it over in her mind for some time, she decided that is what she would plan to do. She just had to make a change in her personnel operation for awhile to get Tyler off her mind and put all of her attention on her business. She could get it all set up for Roger and Betsy and the rest of her crew to handle things at the studio for a week or so while she was gone. She was sure that would work out alright.

She talked to Darcy about her going, and Darcy thought it was a great idea and a chance to get other things straightened out concerning Greg and Rod. Maybe she could decide if she really loved either one of them. She was sure it wasn't real love with Greg, but her feelings for Rod were different. They seemed to be deeper and more sincere.

She got on the phone and made reservations for the following week on a Friday, returning the following Friday. During that time she hadn't heard a word from her sweet Tyler. Then she began to plan on what type of a wardrobe she was going to take. She knew that she had enough to choose from with a lot of her own designs so she wasn't too worried, and maybe she would see something over there that she couldn't live without.

The next day when she got home from the studio, she received a phone call from Rod. "How's my favorite famous designer? Are you alright? I haven't seen or heard from you for weeks now. I read all the notices in the fashion section of the papers and see that you are very busy and becoming very famous. That must make you feel very happy."

Just the fact that he called her made her heart much lighter. "Yes, it does Rod, she responded. I have been getting commissions from some very important people like those in the governmental plus some from Hollywood, and orders are coming in.

"I'm so happy to hear that you are doing so well, darling," he told her. "Do you think that you could squeeze in a little time to go out with me one night?"

"Well Rod, I have decided to go away for a week or two and have a little rest. There has been so much happening here lately, and I thought getting away would be good for me and give me a fresh outlook on things."

"Oh, where did you plan on going? I would like to go with you if you would allow me. Do you think you would?" He asked

"No Rod, this time I would rather go alone. I love your company and being with you, but this time I feel like I should be alone," she answered. "I decided the trip to Paris would solve two problems for me, one is to see if I can broaden my design ideas and the other would be to give me a chance to straighten things out in my personal life. One of the designers there has presented me an invitation, and I feel that it may help me to keep up with the European fabrics and ideas. I have been doing so well since I decided to design my own fabrics, and now I would like to see what I can do with it."

"Well, from what I am reading, you have made it to the top, and you have become the most sought-after designer out there now. I can understand why you want to keep going and not let anyone stand in your way."

"What do you mean by that, Rod?" she asked.

"Well, I have come to the conclusion that you didn't want anyone or anything else in your life, only your design business, and as much as I love you, you don't want me and now I can see why."

She knew in her heart that he wasn't speaking the truth. "Rod, it isn't that I don't want you. You will always be in my heart, but I couldn't find myself in love with you as much as I wanted." I hope that you can also find the love of your life some day. I will always hold you in my heart as a friend and also hold dear the close friendship that we had together. Who knows what is in store for us? Maybe one day we will find each other. Also please convey my thanks and regards to your dear parents when you see them again."

"Will I ever see you again? I would like to, if there isn't someone else," he asked in sort of a sad pleading way.

"I can't tell you right now Rod. I think that I have found someone that I may be falling in love with, but I'm not sure, and he has gone away. I'm hoping that I will see him when I get back to New York in a couple of weeks," she answered.

After pausing and thinking of what she had just told him, he said to her, "Well, I will check with you in a couple of weeks. Take good care of yourself and be happy and have a very successful trip. And Erika—Remember that I love you, and if you ever decide to come back to me, I will be here for you."

"Thank you, Rod, you are very sweet," she answered, and with a sad tone they ended the call.

The next few days were busy ones for Erika as she wanted everything to be in order before she left.

Her fabric salesman, Jack, came in to take an order from her. This was the time she could question him about Tyler. After she gave him her order, it was the perfect time to ask him if he knew or heard anything from Tyler.

He informed her that he hadn't seen or talked to Tyler for weeks. "Why do you ask?" he said.

"Well I saw him several times after we celebrated New Years together, and we had a very loving time together. It was so wonderful for both of us. We made love and discovered that we were in love with one another. He said he loved me and wanted to marry me and wanted me to move my business to California and be with him. He made me promise that I would give him my answer when he returned. We had a date for the following Sunday before he was to leave on Monday. A day or so before that, he called me and seemed very upset and said something very urgent came up, and he had to cancel our date for Sunday. He seemed very disappointed about that and said he would call me later and tell me all about it. I haven't heard from him since, and to tell you the truth, I am very worried about him, and really miss him. I thought you may be able to shine some light on the situation for me."

"No, Erika. I know that if he told you that he loved you and wanted to marry you, he was sincere about it. He is not that kind of a guy. I know that if he tells a girl that he loves her, it is true. He never has strung a girl on. I have known him too long to not be absolutely sure about that. Besides, I don't have any idea what would be a reason for him to make such a call or what would be a reason for him to return to California in such an urgent way. He has nothing or no one there to have a reason to do that. He has no family there or anyone that would need him in a hurry. I am puzzled also."

Then he said to her, "I'll tell you what I will do. When I get to California, I will check and see what I can find out, and if I see him, I will certainly convey your concern for him. If he has forgotten you and wasn't sincere with you, I believe you certainly are entitled to know. I will let you know so that you won't need to worry anymore. I will find out all of the information I can for you about the situation."

"Thank you, Jack, I really do appreciate all your efforts," she said to him.

Then she said, "I feel that I should get away for awhile and get my life straightened out. I had an invitation to go to Paris to check on the fashion exhibition they are having there, so I can perhaps improve my designs. Tyler had mentioned to me that it may be an advantage for me. So I decided that this would be a good time, and it would also keep me busy, and perhaps I can get Tyler off my mind for awhile. I am leaving for Paris Friday and I won't be back until the following Friday, so please if you will, let me know then what you find out Jack, will you?"

He assured her he would and wished her a very good trip and said that he would see her when she got back.

Erika felt a little more at ease since she would have someone at least checking on Tyler, and maybe he would find something out about Tyler's disappearance.

That night, when she arrived at home, Darcy was there, and they talked about the Tyler problem and what had been happening to Erika with Greg and Rod and that Rod told her he loved her and would be there for her if she decided she wanted him. She thought it was pretty well settled with them, that she may be in love with someone else.

"It sounds to me like they are both going to hang in there until they know for sure, and I know that Rod will because I feel that he truly loves you," Darcy told her.

"I hope not because I feel that I may love Tyler and want the love he has for me. Maybe by the time I get back, things will be different. If Tyler is still gone, I might discover that I am in love with Rod; I don't believe that it will be Greg. I believe that Greg has just awakened my sexual desires that have never been awakened before," she said to Darcy.

Darcy just shrugged her shoulders in an undecided manner and walked away.

"Anyway, I hope that I am so busy at the studio that I won't be able to think of my love life anymore."

She continued preparing for her trip, and when Friday came around, she was ready. Darcy went with her to see her off at the airport and wished her a good trip. She hoped that Erika might find a new, real love in Paris. Erika laughed at her remark and boarded the plane.

It was a long flight, and she was very glad she had chosen to go first class.

The party sitting in the seat next to her seemed like a very nice gentleman. He asked if she was from New York, and she said, "No, I am from Pennsylvania but live in New York at the present."

He told her he was from Washington D.C., and he was going to France for a press conference. Then he asked her what her reason for going was, and she told him it was to attend the fashion exhibit there, that she was a fashion designer and wanted to broaden her mind in regards to their fabrics and ideas. Then he asked her how long she intended to be there and she told him, "I must return to my studio in a week as I have commitments to fulfill."

They talked about all sorts of things, like things that were happening in the world. Some of the topics she didn't know much about but would just go along with the conversation. They watched television, enjoyed their meals and their cocktails together. Erika spent a lot of her time sketching and reading magazines.

Soon it was getting close to landing time and the passengers began to stir around preparing for the landing.

Then he asked her if she would have dinner with him some time while she was there.

"Where are you staying?" he asked her.

"I have reservation at the L'Empire Paris Hotel, and I don't know exactly where it is located," she told him.

After thinking about the dinner date and not being too enthused, she said to him, "I won't know my itinerary until I get there and obtain the schedules for the fashion exhibits."

"Well, I can call your hotel and see if you are available. Would you mind that?" he asked.

Since she was not very interested, she answered, "That will be fine if you can catch me in. I will be very busy while I am there."

He assisted her with her luggage, and they prepared to disembark the plane. As they landed, he said, "I will call you at your hotel later if you don't mind. Have a good visit," and they parted.

She took a cab to the hotel and was very aware of how fast the motorists drove their cars in France and it sort of scared her. The cab delivered her to the hotel, and she checked in. She found it to be very modern and charming. She decided that she couldn't have asked for anything better.

After a shower and a changing of attire, she went down to check out where the restaurant and bar were located. While strolling around, she met a few of the French designers who were there, and talked to some of them and found them very interesting. It was very difficult communicating with them because of their different languages. They were from different places. Three of them were from Italy, and two or three were male designers. From them she obtained all the information about the design and fabric exhibitions and where they were going to be held. It was to be for three days, and it opened the next day. She was anxious to see what they had to offer in styles and new fabrics.

After she had some dinner and went back to her room, there was a message there that was left by the gentleman on the plane asking if she would have dinner with him tomorrow evening. She wondered if she should accept his offer; perhaps it might be interesting. He didn't seem to impress her much on the plane, so she decided she didn't want to accept the invitation. She just thought it better not to answer his request and just let it pass.

She attended the exhibition the next day and found it quite interesting. She formed some very good ideas for her designs when she returned to New York. The exhibition was going to be on again the next day, and she planned to attend it again, so she retired very early and thought about Tyler and wondered what he was doing and if Jack had found out anything concerning him. Why couldn't she get him off of her mind she asked herself. She decided that she had to forget about him because he definitely wasn't in love with her or he would have contacted her by now. She finally dozed off to sleep.

The next morning, it was the fashion show again, and she met a few more informative people and got many more ideas. After taking in the show and shopping around in all the boutiques shops, she decided to have dinner and retire early.

The following day was the fashion show once again. She dressed and went down to the lobby to see if there was much commotion. When she went into the show, it didn't seem to be very much different than before so she just walked around to see other things in the same neighbor.

After her dinner, she went up to her room and decided to look over some of the brochures that she had picked up. Tyler was becoming a more remote memory now that she was thinking more of the design work. Then she decided to retire and she dozed off.

Suddenly the phone rang and awakened her. She answered it and the voice on the other end said, "Hello, is this Erika?" The voice sounded quite familiar, and she immediately thought it was the gentleman from the plane calling again, but it had a French accent.

"Yes it is," she answered.

"Well, we have a wire for you from the United States. Would you like us to bring it up or would you prefer to pick it up at the front desk?" he asked.

"I will be right down to pick it up," she informed him. She hurriedly dressed and took the elevator down, wondering who would send her a wire. She hoped that Darcy was alright and that there were no problems at the studio

When she picked it up and read it, she found that it was from Jack, her fabric salesman. It read, "Have info on Tyler. Stop address from room-mate Stop your return? Stop. What is next step? Stop. Jack."

She inquired from the desk as to how she could send an answer and how long it would take to get back there. He said he could help her, and it would probably get back there the next day. So she answered Jack the next morning and told him that she would be back there in about three to four days and, "Keep it safe for me until I return. Thank you, Jack."

The next day was the last day of the exhibit so she spent the whole day taking in all the French knowledge that she possibly could. She was pleased at what she already had gotten. She located another fabric source from Italy that she liked and knew she could use so she ordered some fabrics.

Chapter 7
THE UNEXPECTED

The following day was open for her. There was no fashion show, so she decided that she would see some of the things in Paris that she had read about many times. She asked the concierge at the desk about some tours, and he gave her some good directions. She spent the whole day seeing things that she never imagined she would ever see, like the Eiffel Tower and the Arch de Triumph and many more things of interest to her. It was a long tour, and when she returned to the hotel, she was pretty tired, but she realized that she wasn't in a sad mood about Tyler. Maybe Jack had some good news for her, she thought, and that eased her mind a bit.

When she got to her room, she took a shower and dressed and went down for dinner. At the restaurant she met a couple of the designers, and they talked all about the styles in France and Italy. She found them very interesting. Even though they had a language barrier, she could understand them pretty well.

The next morning when she went down to the lobby, she found a cute outdoor café off to the side of the lobby and decided she would have breakfast there. It seemed so cheery. She sat there watching the people go by with all of their different types of dress. Some of them were pretty revealing, she thought. It seemed that was the mode of dress there. Surprisingly, she admired some of the outfits. She was seeing so many types and styles of dressing that it didn't surprise her much.

She watched for awhile longer and noticed she was seeing so many military men, and most of them were from America. She discovered later that they were on their way back home from the war that had ended earlier.

Then her thoughts went to Rod and Greg and she thought to herself, maybe I should go back and be fair with them and see if I could be in love with either one of them. I do think a lot of them, and they both kind of excite me, Rod especially, and he is so secure and has so much more love and concern for me. I think Greg just awakened my sexual desires. Would that be fair to them? After all she did know that they loved her, but it would be like taking one of them as a second choice. Maybe she had better wait and see if she would find someone else whom she could truly love more. All of this was going through her mind.

Then she asked herself, why am I so intent on finding someone I love who would love me as much as I think Tyler did. I have my business that I always dreamed of, and I should put all of my thoughts on that. Every so often Rod popped up in her mind, and the thought of him caressing her gave her a thrill. She remembered how wonderful he was to her. But then her mind went back to Tyler. So on and on—she thought about everything.

She was just taking the last sip of her espresso and looked up casually and was absolutely shocked. She thought perhaps she was seeing things. There were so many military men walking around, and they all seemed to look alike. As she kept watching, there appeared a gentleman walking quite a ways from her, but toward her, and he looked exactly like Tyler.

Then she thought-—that cannot be Tyler. The man resembles him, but it couldn't be him, what would he be doing way over here? Am I thinking about him so much that I see him in other men? She blinked and looked at him again. When she did, she saw him come closer to her with a beautiful smile directed at her. She had to blink several times because she didn't believe her eyes. Was this really her Tyler? But there he was in real life, right next to her. She felt weak in the knees and thought she would faint. He must have known that, because he grabbed her and held her so close she could hardly breathe.

Finally the tears just came pouring out of her eyes. "Where did you come from and how in the world did you find me over here?" she asked.

"Darling did you ever think that I could not find you wherever you went. You could never get lost from me. I will find you wherever you are; you are part of my heart and will always be there," he said as he embraced her and kissed her lovingly on the lips. She wasn't conscious of any one around them. She didn't care now—she had her Tyler. She just wanted to cling to him so he could not leave her again

He said, "I couldn't wait for you to come back. I wanted you now. So I took the first plane out as soon as Jack told me where you were. It took me a whole day to find you here.

"But Tyler, what happened? Why didn't you contact me? I thought you went out of my life forever and found someone else. I thought I would never see you again," she said.

"Darling, there is nothing in this world that could keep me away from you forever. If I told you that I loved you and wanted you, I meant exactly that. I will explain everything to you when we get to the room," he said to her. She stayed as close to him as she could until they got to her room. She couldn't believe that he was there at her side.

When they stepped inside, he grabbed her and embraced her like he would never let her go. "Oh my darling, I never intended to hurt you, and when the urgent call came to me, I didn't have a chance to explain. I will explain now and hope and pray that you will understand and still love me as I believe you did before."

He went on to tell her that, as she already knew, he was in the import business and was the owner of three different factories in Asia and had lots of shipments of his fabrics going out constantly. Then the authorities got word that there was a package in one of his shipments that was some kind of drugs, so they confiscated a package from one of his shipments and discovered that it was heroin. They formed the idea that he was trying to get heroin into the United States. They immediately put out a warrant for his arrest, and they picked him up in California as soon as he arrived. He was incarcerated and couldn't make any calls. They put his import license on hold and continued to hold him until they could prove it wasn't him and caught the one who did it. They kept everything sort of hush-hush while they investigated it thoroughly. Until they could catch the culprit, they held him.

Finally, after a couple of months, they caught the guy. He worked for another importer and found out that Tyler had shipments coming to the States regularly. When the authorities checked to see who the shipments were coming to, they caught the culprits on both sides.

"I couldn't be released until they were sure they had the sender and the receiver. I was going crazy worrying about leaving you like I did," Tyler said. Then Jack contacted me and told me that you had talked to him and what you said to him. As soon as I was released, I called your studio, and they told me you were out of town, but they didn't tell me where. Then Jack told me where you had gone, and I tried to get the first flight I could, and it wasn't easy, but I did. I waited in New York for the first flight over here. I was so afraid that someone else would win your heart, and I would lose you. I was going crazy. Could you ever find it in your heart to forgive me, my darling?" He looked at her with saddened eyes and waited for her answer.

Instead, she engulfed his head in her hands and pressed it to her breast and said to him, "Tyler, I was so worried about your safety, and I'm happy that you are alright and not hurt. I know you truly love me and wouldn't do that intentionally. Of course I forgive you, but you must promise you will never leave me like that again."

When she said that, he reached into his pocket and came out holding a silver box and asked her to open it. When she did, she was shocked and could not believe her eyes at what she saw. It was a gorgeous diamond ring with a large diamond in the center and blue sapphires surrounding it. She had never seen anything that beautiful and she started to cry. "No, don't cry my darling. When I saw that ring I thought of you on our first date on New Year's Eve, and you wore that gown. It reminded me of you and how beautiful you looked that night. You are meant to have that ring. Always remember me with it."

As he slipped it on her finger, he said, "Now you are promised to me and we belong to one another." He embraced her and pressed his very warm lips on hers and picked her up and carried her to the bedroom. Slowly he disrobed her and looked at her beautiful body and decided it was the body of an angel, and now it was his. He couldn't refrain from kissing that soft body all over. Then she was in heaven just as she was the first night that they were together.

He continued kissing and finally she said to him "Tyler, do you still want an answer from me for that big question you asked me before you left?"

"I most certainly do, have you decided?" he asked.

"Yes I did and, my answer is yes, as soon as we get back to New York. Being separated from you this time I realized how much I care for you."

She continued, "And about the request you had for me to go to California with you, I've decided I will open another studio out there and have both places to operate my design business. I feel now that the way my business is going and coming from all directions that it shouldn't make any difference. I have been accepting many requests from the studios there, and my business is building in the West also."

He tightened his embrace on her and lovingly kissed her all over— her eyes, her neck and down to her breasts. He was so happy to know that she cared that much for him, and she was so happy to have him in her arms and know that he also really loved her.

They spent a lot of the night making plans for her to open another studio in California, and the more Erika thought about being with Tyler forever she decided she didn't care where she would be as long as Tyler was with her. She wanted someone to love her that much.

Meanwhile, back in New York, Darcy had sent a letter to Erika telling her all about things happening back there. She was seeing her friend, Brad, and falling more in love with him as time went on. She said that she had accepted Brad's proposal of marriage, and the wedding was planned for June. She was very anxious for Erika to return as she wanted her to be in the wedding as her bride's maid, and she wanted her to design their wedding gowns. She told Erika that she was selling more jewelry at her job at the jewelry store and was making more great commissions, and she was doing great.

She also informed Erika that Rod's and Greg's thoughts were still on Erika. She said that they were still checking occasionally to see when she was coming back. She told her that Rod had been dating the interior decorator that helped him with the décor in his new apartment, but he continued to call every other day asking about Erika. She also told Erika that she believed Rod really loved her. Greg was seeing the agent he met at the other real estate office. It seems they both have found solace with each other for the time being, but Greg is not forgetting about Erika. She told Erika that she really missed her and hoped that she was having a good time and not letting the thought of Tyler spoil her trip. She said to go and see lots of the sights in France while she was there.

She said that she was looking forward to Erika returning home on Friday. She missed her and was anxious to tell her about getting married to Brad and about help with her wedding gown. She wanted to hear all about what she found out about Tyler.

When Darcy got home from work Friday, she expected to see Erika there that evening, but instead she had a wire waiting for her. Opening it she read: Tyler and I to marry. Stop Seeing the country. Stop. Be back next Friday. Stop. Clue you in later. Stop. Tell Roger &Betsy & Rod back next Friday. Stop Wishes to you &Brad.

Back in Paris, Tyler and Erika decided that they would spend the seven days they had left together on some recreation and celebrate their engagement. They decided that when they got back to New York, Erika would be required to concentrate on the large work orders that were piling up there, and they would have very little time to be together then.

Tyler thought it would be very nice to rent a car and travel to some of the other places that would be interesting to see while they were there. Erika thought that was a very good idea, and she could use the relaxation before the stress at the studio. So they rented a car and took off to see other places. Tyler had never been to Europe before but often thought that he would like to go, and since he was there now, he might as well see some places other than just Paris.

Due to the schedule that Erika had, they would only be able to see what they could in close proximity to Paris. So they headed southwest toward an area where Tyler discovered was all vineyards. He had read about them and all the areas where they could be located. Some of them were southwest of Paris. If they wanted to stay overnight, they could stay at a hotel right there close to the vineyards. While driving along and enjoying the beautiful scenery they noticed that there were vineyards in many areas.

They spent a lot of time discussing their future and their coming marriage. Tyler said he thought he would like to get married as soon as they got back to New York, and he chose to have the ceremony at the 21 Club because that was the first big date he had with Erika. Erika said she chose to be married in a church, but she didn't know which church yet.

After going back and forth over it, they decided to compromise and have the wedding in a church and have a reception at the 21 Club. Then Tyler reached over and kissed her on the cheek. "You are so understanding, my sweet Erika. You certainly know how to compromise." All of their discussions were while they were driving.

When they had driven almost all day, Tyler said, "I think we are going to stay at a hotel in the next town. We'll look for a nice hotel and spend the night there and start out early in the morning. What do you think, darling?"

"I think that will be great as long as you think we can get back to Paris In time," she said to him. "That is no problem," he told her.

So in a very short time they came to the town and started to look for a hotel. It wasn't long until they found one that looked good to them. They also noticed that there was a small winery close by and decided that they would visit that the following day. They had a delicious French dinner and departed to find their rooms. Erika decided that she didn't want to share a room with Tyler. She wanted to save her love until they were man and wife. That is what she was brought up to believe in her religion. Tyler was very unhappy about that but finally agreed. They both knew that they would sleep as soon as they made it to the bed. But that didn't happen for Tyler, as he wanted to be with Erika and love her all night.

The next morning they started out for the big winery that they were headed for initially.

When they arrived, the tour was just going out. The wine tasting had begun, and the visitors were having tastes of different aperitifs before following the guide on the tour of the winery. After that it was dinner time. After dinner they tasted different types of wine, and then it was time to retire to their hotel.

It was a charming hotel, and the rooms were decorated in the French motif which Erika found very interesting. She had never seen anything like it before. Again she insisted on separate rooms, and again Tyler was disappointed.

He decided that he would leave wake-up calls for them in the morning.

The phone rang with the wake-up call, and Tyler went to wake up Erika. He told Erika how disappointed he was not being able to hold her and caress her in the night. She gave him a sweet kiss on the lips and said," Don't worry, dear Tyler, we will have plenty of time for that after we are married."

They had their breakfast, got in the car and started back. As they talked about what they had already seen and the country they saw, Tyler said to her, "What do you think about us taking a different route back to Paris? We could see something new and probably get back there sooner."

It didn't make any difference to her, so she answered, "Darling, you are the engineer and I am the passenger, and if you want to go a different way, it is up to you." They laughed about her calling him an engineer. So, he decided to go to back through Tours and then to Paris. That seemed to be a shorter route.

He planned on them stopping for lunch in Tours and staying overnight there and then on to Paris the next day. That would get them back in plenty of time for their flight. He stopped to fill up with fuel for the third time since leaving Paris. Erika was enjoying the sights they were seeing and mentioned it to Tyler. Then he said to her, "If you are enjoying these sights, you would really enjoy seeing California. There are so many sights there you wouldn't believe it."

"Is that true, my darling? Well, I guess I will have to go out there and see with my own eyes, don't you think?" she said to him with a laugh. "I certainly do think that," he answered her and squeezed her arm. "We'll see," she retorted.

They were talking so much and Tyler didn't realize how far he had gone already so he suggested that it was about time to have some lunch. So Tyler found a cute sidewalk café, and they had a very nice lunch. Afterwards, it was on to Tours to overnight there. The weather was getting cooler, and Erika wrapped her sweater around her to be a little warmer.

When they had driven about another hour, the road became a little more treacherous with curves and narrow shoulders. Erika mentioned it to Tyler and he said to her, "Please don't worry, darling, I think I can handle driving on this type of a road. I have had experience driving roads like this in Asia." That seemed to calm Erika down, but she still was a little nervous. Tyler tried to keep Erika from thinking about the road by talking to her.

After driving about thirty more minutes, they both heard a lot of tires screeching, and all of a sudden, she felt Tyler put on the brakes and the car skid. Erika screamed. There was a horrible crash and the sound of metal to metal and the breaking of glass, and it seemed to her that they were falling in the air, and then everything went blank for her.

Erika seemed to be in an abyss and was hearing an echo of someone calling, "Rod, Rod, Rod, I can't see you, I can't see you, come and help me, I need you." Who was that lady calling for Rod? Why isn't he with her? He was always there when she needed him. Then everything went black, and she was back in that abyss. Soon she heard someone calling out, "Tyler, where are you? Are you alright?" She didn't hear anything else after. Then she saw lights glaring in her eyes and smelled the awful odor of ether. She heard someone saying, "Lady, do you hear me, can you open your eyes?" Then there was silence again.

She was so weak now, and all she wanted to do was go back to that black hole. She wasn't aware of the time, but the next thing she knew, someone was asking her to open her eyes again. She tried but she just couldn't seem to open them. When she finally did get them open, what she saw scared her more. She saw doctors and nurses standing around her bed, and she realized that she had all kinds of medical tubes attached to her. "Where am I?" she asked.

The doctor spoke up and said, "Ma'am, you are in a hospital. You were in an automobile accident, and they brought you here a few days ago. We will keep you here until we get you patched up."

Erika became very distraught and asked, "Where is Tyler? Where is Tyler?" Then her head seemed to spin around, and everything became black, and she went back into that hole. She didn't know how long she was out, but when she was able to open her eyes, she called for Tyler again

The lady in white asked her, "Who is Rod? When you were delirious you repeatedly called out for Rod and Tyler? Who is Tyler? Who was with you in the car? Was Rod or Tyler with you?"

Erika came to the conclusion that this was a nurse, and she answered her in a very weak voice, "Yes, Tyler was with me. Is he here? I want to see him. Is he alright?" She could feel the bandages all over her, and she was very groggy, and her head was hurting. "What is wrong with me, and how did I get here? Where am I hurt? My head hurts. I want to see Tyler," she said through her tears.

Then the doctor appeared holding a syringe and gave her an injection in her arm and said to her, "You must rest now, and when you wake up, we will see where Tyler is."

Later, a nurse was at her bedside calling her name. "Miss Beiler,

Miss Beiler, can you hear me?" and Erika looked up at the nurse and answered very weak voice, "Yes I am awake. How long have I been here? Please tell me what happened, and where is Tyler? I want to see Tyler."

The nurse looked at her and asked, "Is Tyler the gentleman who was with you in the car?" Erika gave her a slightly affirmative nod, as her head was still hurting.

Then the nurse took her hand and said, "You have been here three days, and I am so sorry but the gentleman was fatally injured and did not make it. He passed away after they brought him here."

Erika cried out, "Oh, no!" The nurse could see the heavy tears rolling down her cheeks, and she could hardly control the sobbing. "You are very lucky to be here. We had a difficult time saving you, with all the injuries that you had. We thought at first it was a fractured skull and a broken neck, but it was just a very bad gash on your head causing a concussion and a dislocated collar bone. One of your legs is fractured but we are sure that it will be alright with a little time."

Her heart was breaking for poor Tyler. She said to the nurse in a quivering voice, "We were to be married," and showed her the ring, which was still on her finger where Tyler placed it.

"Oh, Miss, I am so sorry. Who is Rod? Is he someone we should contact? Is there someone you would like us to notify of your accident? I don't know if the police notified anyone since the accident or not."

Erika thought a minute and decided that she didn't want them to notify Rod. She didn't want him to know yet. She wasn't ready to let him know how much she needed him. It seemed that she always needed him, whenever there was a problem. So she said to the nurse, "Could you please notify my roommate, and she will take care of it from there."

So Erika gave her all the information she would need to contact Darcy. What about Tyler? She thought, she didn't have any idea as who to notify, and she said this to the nurse. She started to cry again and it seemed like she couldn't stop. She had lost Tyler before she ever got to know or really love him, she thought. He was such a sweet man. She cried for him again.

The next day, the nurse came in and told her that they had notified Darcy via wire, but they hadn't heard anything from her as yet. Erika just laid there in her hospital bed and kept thinking of Tyler and all the things that they had planned. Poor Tyler, why did this have to happen to him? His life ended so soon.

The following day, while she lay there thinking, her thought drifted to Rod and Greg. Maybe she was being punished for the way she passed them off for Tyler. Rod loved her so much. Was God punishing her for that? Why did she do that? They were such very nice gentlemen, and she felt so secure with Rod, and she knew he really loved her. How did she think that she could ever be without him? She always needed him. Her thoughts would keep going back to the Christmas vacation they had together and how badly he wanted her. Why did she reject his love? She asked herself. She could easily have been receptive to it. She cared for him that much

When the doctor came in to see her that day, she asked him about Tyler again, and that was when he told her that someone had made arrangements to send him back to the United States, but he couldn't tell her who it was.

He removed the bandage from her head where it had a bad gash. It was healing and just needed a smaller bandage. She was very happy that they didn't have to cut off her hair, just a little patch on the top. It was a deep gash but not very big. That's why when they brought her in at first they thought she had a fractured skull. He told her that he had several calls inquiring about her, but he couldn't tell who the calls were from either.

Then he informed her, "Your injuries are coming along fine so far. You will need to wear a neck brace and a cast on your leg for awhile, but you should be released in less than a week. I understand that you and the gentleman with you in the car were planning to be married"

"Yes, as soon as we returned to the States—we had it all planned." Again the salty tears rolled down her cheeks as she thought about her poor Tyler. When the doctor left her room, she laid back and dozed off as there wasn't much she could do. She didn't have the ambition to do any drawing, and it would be very inconvenient to do that while she was reclined in the bed. Everything she thought about made her feel sad, and she cried. The nurses were very nice to her, and when they brought her lunch or dinner, they always asked if there was something else that they could get for her. She really didn't have much appetite, but they insisted that she eat some of it to give her strength, which she generally tried to do.

On the fifth day there, after her lunch, they came in and propped her up in a slight sitting position, and she tried to read a little to keep her mind off of things. She thought about Rod and how much he loved her. She wanted to love him the same way. Would she ever love him that much? She worried about the studio and if Roger and Betsy were running things OK and if the orders were getting out. She knew she was going to need to contact them very soon.

She was looking at a French fashion magazine, and she found some very interesting things in it. She was so engrossed in what she was reading that she didn't hear anyone enter her room. Suddenly, there was a shadow crossing the page, and she felt someone there so she looked up and her mouth fell wide open. She thought she must be delirious, but there stood Rod in real life, as handsome as ever. She was so happy to see him. He looked so good to her.

After feeling so alone in this country without anyone she knew and losing someone she cared for, she was ready for someone to fill that empty space in her heart—someone who really loved her.

Heavy tears began to roll again, and she threw open her raised arms in a motion that invited his embrace. His eyes started to well up, and he embraced her gently and said, "My sweet Erika, I just had to come. I couldn't bear the thought of you being here all alone suffering with no one to really care. I'm sorry for what has happened to you and all of your plans, but I always told you how much I loved you and would always be there for you. I came as soon as Darcy let me know. I couldn't get here fast enough. Now I want you to get well enough to go back with me. I want to take care of you. I love you so much and can't bear to see you suffer."

"Oh Rod, you have always been so wonderful to me. I realize now how much I always needed you. I really need to get back to my studio and take care of that also. It has always been my dream, and I don't want to lose it now."

Then he told her that he had talked to Roger and Betsy, and they said for her to get well, that everything was going good. He also said Darcy sent her love and wished her a quick recovery. Getting that little bit of news did wonders for Erika's spirits. She made up her mind then that she was going to get well enough for her flight back home as soon as possible even if she had to fly with her bandages and cast.

Rod said to her, "Darling I am staying here with you until you are well enough to go back with me, and I will never let you go again."

The doctors told her that they were sure she could leave the hospital in a few days. She would be required to wear the cast on her leg and the brace on her neck, but otherwise she should be OK to travel.

As soon as the doctors released her and gave her all the instructions as how to care for herself and insisted that she see her doctor as soon as she reached New York, she and Rod left the hospital. They headed back to Paris to get her luggage at the hotel, and then they boarded the plane together for New York. Oh, how great it felt to have Rod at her side and be heading back to her studio.

Rod was a prince with her on the way back. He helped her with everything, and her heart went out to him for all of his efforts and inconveniences. She wanted to kiss and embrace him several times but refrained from that. Why didn't she follow her desires with him? Why was she resisting the love that he so desperately wanted to give her? Why didn't she realize that before all of this happened? She asked herself.

He made sure that there was a wheelchair there for transporting her around. He saw that she was very comfortable in her seat and that she was warm enough and had enough to eat. He took care of her like a baby.

Finally, they were back in New York, and Darcy met them at the airport and delivered them to Rod's apartment. That is where he wanted to take her so he could be with her until she got well. He didn't think that she should go to the studio until she was better.

He insisted on getting a maid in to help her until she could get around without the splint. She didn't want that, but he finally won with his decision. He had all the conveniences for her that he thought she needed, and he was there every day to see that she was well taken care of. He loved her and was eager for her to get well. He couldn't wait to give her his love.

She was there with him for more than a month, and as the days passed she found Tyler would only be in her mind occasionally. Rod was giving her all the affection and care she needed. He kissed her passionately whenever he had the opportunity, and she was beginning to be more receptive and desirous of his love.

After being with him all that time, she became more attracted to him, and her feelings were growing into deeper love. Every time he caressed her or kissed her, she was becoming desirous of his love and wanted to give him all that she had stored up for him for so long. The longer she was with him, the more she wanted him.

The doctors had removed her neck brace earlier and said it would soon be time to remove her leg cast. She was so happy and couldn't wait until it was off. Rod was elated. It had been on since the accident. The morning that it was to come off, he said to her, "My darling I'm looking forward to holding you so very close to me and giving you all my love. I can't wait." Erika found that in her heart she was looking forward to that also, and she started to tingle all over, even down to the one leg that had the cast on it.

She was very anxious to get back to the studio. Rod had taken her there several times while she had the cast on, but she felt that she should be there more to see that all was going well. So, as soon as she could, she planned to be there.

When her cast was off, Rod took her back to his place again. Then she said to him, "Rod, I think it is time for me to go home to my own apartment, don't you?" Deep inside, she knew she didn't want to leave him. She was so happy being close to him. Putting his arms around her, he said, "Darling I don't want you to go. I need you here with me. I have always wanted you with me since the day I met you."

After having the cast removed, and they returned to his apartment, she thought how wonderful it would feel to have a nice refreshing shower, and she couldn't wait to have that warm water splashing over her. It felt so good to have that cast off and to feel that warm shower on her whole body. When she stepped out of the shower, Rod was there to hand her a towel. He couldn't take his eyes away from her body. Then he said to her, "Oh my darling, I feel just as I did the day at my parent's home, when you stepped out of the showers with your body shimmering wet and your beautiful long hair cascading down your wet body. You are so beautiful. I want to embrace you and love you like I have wanted since that day."

He was embracing her nude body tightly and kissing her all over her face and neck. She began to get the feeling that she had when he removed the robe from her body, and it fell to the floor in the bedroom of his parents' home. She was tingling all over now. He continued to kiss her passionately moving downward with his warm lips on her soft skin, until he found her firm breasts. She was becoming ecstatic and oblivious of all things. Now she was ready to give him all the love that she had pent up inside of her since she first met him. She knew that deep inside, she had always wanted him, but resisted. She had always been attracted to him but rejected the love he had for her. Now she was ready to remove those barriers and submitted eagerly. He said to her quietly, "My Darling Erika, this is what I have been dreaming about ever since I met you. Why have you resisted me so long?" She couldn't answer that and wondered herself, why she had, when she was sure she loved him all along since the day he showed her his apartment, and she was so attracted to him then. Now releasing all the feelings that she had for him, she knew that she loved him.

"Oh my dearest Erika, you are making me the happiest man on earth. I want to marry you and have you with me forever. If you would say you will marry me, my darling, that would make my life complete. You know that the day I met you I knew you were meant for me. Do you remember that? I even said that to my mother." Erika did remember him telling her that.

She thought to herself, "Was it possible that she always wanted Rod's love but was afraid that his love wasn't sincere enough for her to reciprocate,? Had she stored it all up inside and released it on Tyler, because she really wanted Rod to love that way? Could that have been the reason she went to someone else for the love she wanted? Tyler was a sweet man, just as Rod, and it was easy for her to release it on him. She would always remember Tyler and how dear he was with her,

All the while that Rod was making love to her, he was asking her to please marry him. He pleaded with her, "Erika, you know that I have loved you and wanted you since that day that I met you and showed you my apartment. I have felt all along that we are soul mates, and I really want to marry you and have you be mine. Do you think that you could say yes to me? I want to give you my heart and have you with me forever," he pleaded as he peered deep into her eyes.

Erika said to him, "My darling Rod, in these past months, with all the anguish that we have had and the love and care that you have given me, I really believe that I have finally come to realize that it is you I really love. I think I loved you all along and didn't want to let you know. I looked for you near me whenever I needed someone. I believe that I wanted you so much that when Tyler came into my life, I accepted him with the love that I wanted from you. I believe we are soul-mates. Why did I call out for you when I was delirious in the hospital? They told me that I kept calling out your name. Subconsciously, I believe you were foremost in my mind because I really loved you. Darling Rod, I want to be your wife. I know I love you and would love to be Mrs. Rod Burton."

While still embracing her nude body, he tightened his embrace and didn't want to let her go. He wanted to give her more of his love. This time she wanted and accepted him as he reclined her body. She didn't push him away from her as she had before—this time she wanted more of him. His love made her feel ecstatic. She knew that she always wanted him but never dreamed that being loved by him would be so wonderful.

His warm lips were moving all over her body and her tingling became maddening, She didn't reject him as he entered her and their bodies became one, but she gave to him completely. They were both in heaven now. Rod kept stoking her beautiful, long, blond hair as they continued with their caressing and love. They gave to each other completely until they were spent, then cuddled in each other's arms and slept.

Chapter 8
THE RIGHT ROAD

When they awoke the next morning there was a short repeat of the night before. Rod embraced her, caressed her and she was full of love for him until they finally decided to rise from their love nest.

Erika began to think about the studio and Darcy and the wedding. After speaking to Rod about that, he asked her if she would like him to take her to the studio or her apartment. He suggested that if she went to her apartment, he definitely would want her to come back to his place.

While she was deciding whether to go to the studio or her apartment, she had an idea—she would like to make a nice romantic candle-light dinner for her and Rod to celebrate their love for each other, so she declined his offer

After he kissed her and went out the door to his office, she sat down and made a list of what she would need for the evening's occasion and decided she would go down to the local market and purchase the items.

She was just going out of the door to his apartment and the phone rang.

She imagined that it would be Rod calling her so she picked it up and answered it with, "Hello"

Sounding like a female the caller said, "Hello is Rod there?" "No he isn't he has left for his office. Who is calling and may I give him a message?"

Without stating a name, the woman said, "This is his fiancé, and who is this speaking?"

Erika was so shocked that she couldn't answer her question instead she informed the caller that she must have the wrong number.

"No I do not have the wrong number, I have dialed this number many times and I'm sure this is Rod Burton's phone number. May I ask what are you doing in his apartment?"

Erika felt like a ton of bricks had fallen on her, she was so shocked

Finally she said to the caller, "Well you see, I am Rod Burton's fiancé and we are planning to marry so I think you had better give me some explanations as to what is going on here."

"I don't believe you, and I don't think I need to give you any explanations. Don't you think that the explanations should come from Rod?" the caller informed her.

"You are absolutely right in saying that. If you and Rod are engaged to marry, would you tell me just how long you two have been engaged?" Erika asked

When Erika asked her that—She had a thought come into her mind; was this the Interior Designer that Rod had been seeing, when she had just arrived to New York City? But he told her that he had broken up with her and wasn't seeing her anymore. Was he lying to her or what?

So Erika listened as the caller went on with her story and said, "Well I have known Rod for quite some time and we had been seeing each other for about two years occasionally, in which time he asked me to decorate his new apartment. After that, we sort of drifted apart and I had the feeling that he had found someone new."

She continued with her story—"About four or five months ago, he called me and asked if I would consider seeing him again and I accepted as I was in love with him from the time we first met. After seeing each other frequently, he asked me if I would ever consider marriage and I said yes."

"We continued seeing each other and I expected to see him over the holidays but he didn't call me. Then all of a sudden, his calls discontinued and when I called his office they told me that he was out of the office for the holidays and I left a message. I still didn't hear from him. Then after several weeks of not hearing from him, I called and they told me he was out of the country and wouldn't return for several weeks. I haven't heard from him since and he hasn't answered my calls at home or at the office."

In a bewildered state, Erika listened to her story and finally said to her, "I'll tell you what, I'll give your message to Rod and I'm sure he will call you. What did you say your name was?"

"My name is Myra Sheldon" the caller answered

"Well, my name is Erika and I wish you good luck with your problem" she said to the caller.

"Thank you Erika and good luck to you also" Myra said as she hung up the phone.

After that shocking phone call, Erika didn't know what to do, she was so bewildered.

Then she decided that she would go ahead with the dinner, and at that time she could talk to Rod and find out what that was all about. Her elation of the marriage plans had left her by that time. She couldn't think of going ahead with a marriage to Rod after a shock like that.

Erika prepared the beautiful candle-light dinner and when Rod came home, he was very surprised to see the romantic set-up. He embraced and kissed her and with a glint in his eyes he said, "What is all of this? I thought you would be at the studio?"

"Why don't we sit down and enjoy the dinner I have prepared and then I will tell you what this is all about."Erika said to him.

After they had finished their dinner and talked about other things Rod said, "OK My Darling, now what is this that you wanted to tell me?"

After a deep breath she started, "Well after you left this morning the phone rang and I answered it, thinking that it was you calling me. I realize now, that I shouldn't have answered it."

Erika went on to say, "The caller was someone who claimed that she was your Fiancé.

Needless to say, I was shocked, knowing that you had just proposed to me and that I had accepted."

"She informed me that she was the one who decorated your apartment and you both became very close and finally you had a romantic affair and you asked her to marry you. After trying to reach you by phone several times and leaving messages, you failed to answer her calls."

"Now I'm undecided about our relationship. Can you tell me what this is all about Rod?" She asked him.

Rod sat there embarrassed with a blank look on his face and didn't seem to be able to say a word. Then he began to speak in an attempt to give her his explanation.

"Darling, you know how much I love you and want to marry you, and I can understand your bewilderment with this other person calling you and telling all of this to you.

She and I did have something together but I had already fallen in love with you before my second encounter with her."

When you left me and went away and found someone else, I was devastated and couldn't handle that. I wanted someone to fill up the empty feeling that I got from losing you. I called her and we did see each other often after that."

"She and I did discuss marriage but I never came out and asked her to be my wife. I just asked her if she ever considered marriage and she said yes and we didn't discuss it any further. I'm sorry if she took that as a proposal. I didn't answer her calls because I didn't feel that I wanted to continue our relationship, as I found that I was madly in love with you and I just couldn't put you out of my mind and heart. I believe now, that I should have told her at that time, how I felt."

Erika had been so sure in their past relationship, that Rod had been truthful and candid about himself, but now could she be sure that he was. She was sure that he loved her and was truthful with her now but—could she trust him and would he always be candid with her?

Did she want to give up her dream of being a famous fashion designer under the circumstances that she is experiencing at this time?

She said to him, "Rod, I came here to New York to follow my dream and it seems that I became sidetracked and followed cupid down another road. I feel that I must get back on track if I want to fulfill my dream. I am almost there and I don't want to lose it now."

"My up-bringing with an Amish heritage did not prepare me for the traumatic experiences that I have encountered in this big city, but it did prepare me with perseverance and determination to follow my dream and see that it is fulfilled."

"I have a lot of work to do at the studio and it appears like there is much more of it coming in at this time. I also want to finish Darcy's wedding gown, her wedding will be soon and I promised her I would have it ready for her."

"But Darling, what about our plans, you said that you loved me and wanted to marry me, have you given up on us completely?" Rod pleaded.

Rod, I think the first thing that you had better do is call Myra and get that situation with her straightened out, don't you?"

"Your right, Darling." he agreed

Erika felt that she had to make Rod understand that she couldn't go through with the marriage to him and what her feelings were now, so she said to him, "Rod, my heart tells me that you are my love but the determination to follow my dream pulls me in that direction and I'm afraid that is what I must do. I must put my attention on the fulfilling of my dream and when I find that I have achieved my goal and you are still at my side, then and not until then, can I accept your proposal. Can you understand that?"

Rod embraced her and looked directly into her eyes and said, "My Darling, as I told you before, I love you and will always be there for you and if that is what you want, I will be there with you all the way."

Rod had a very strong feeling that it wouldn't be too long a wait for her to reach her goal as she was doing so well already.

Their conversation ended in agreement by both parties.

Erika immediately started working hard on her Design work and the orders were coming in rapidly. She was putting in many hours of work each day, tirelessly and seemed to thrive on it.

Now, Erika was where she really wanted to be, in her own studio with the orders flowing in. She had completed Darcy's wedding gown and it was beautiful as was the wedding and Brad and Darcy were off on their honeymoon.

When she arrived at the studio one morning to check on how things were progressing she noticed a request to be commissioned for a gown to be designed for the Oscar Award festivities and worn by a prominent star. She was elated and accepted it immediately.

She was planning her own Fashion Show in a couple of weeks and had many new designs to show this time. This would be her very first Fashion Show of her very own.

She could see the wheels of her dream turning rapidly and the fulfillment of it right in front of her eyes.

* * * * * *

More than a year had pasted since the phone encounter with Myra Sheldon and that was history now.

By this time she had presented several Fashion shows that were very successful and was a benefit to her work.

Erika's work had skyrocketed and she had to expand her work spaces and her complete staff. She now occupied a full building and her work staff went from four to twenty-five or more. She also brought in her sister Rachel from her home in Lancaster, to work for her. Rachel had always wanted to join Erika and now she could.

Erika had reached her goal and she was delighted. She was known all over the world now and her designs were shown in all the fashion publications.

Rod was at her side all through her escalating time and she loved him more for that. She would see him as often as she could if it did not interfere with her work.

She had really fulfilled her dream and was on the top of the fashion world. It was her world now but was her world complete she thought, No—not until she had her life-long partner and the man that she loved in marriage and a family that she wanted, which would make her life complete.

She knew in her heart that it wouldn't be much longer and she would be ready to accept Rod as her life-long partner in love and marriage. He was her love and soul-mate and stood by her in reaching the goal of her childhood dream.

This was her world now the world of, **"Creations by Erika"** and love.

About the Author

Claire Gilbert was born in Pennsylvania and traveled to California as a teenager to find her niche in life. She explored several careers before becoming an Interior Designer. Many decades later she retired to Hawaii with her family and began to write fiction. She continues to write and finds it very gratifying.